PROJECT REVERSE
VOL. I: THE HEART SHOP

Illustrations copyright © 2023 by Xii

Cover design by Xii

ISBN 978-629-98383-0-2

First edition 2023

Published by

Xii
32000 Sitiawan,
Perak,
Malaysia

Printed by One Heart Print

project-reverse.com

PROLOGUE

Twenty-five miles from Creave, located between a town and a city, was a vibrant night stop for tourists, hipsters, and partygoers. The skies of the main streets boasted crowded neon signboards and gold-red lanterns reminiscent of faraway places. Restaurants, dance clubs, and pubs took up most of the business spots, growing exponentially from abundant sales. The surrounding shops benefited from the prime location as well.

Along one of the narrower backstreets, a young lady stood, staring up at an unusual shop that loomed above her. The merry sounds of the street were muffled. The only thing she heard was her own heart racing against possibilities.

She had been staring at the sign hanging at eye level for the past ten minutes.

The Heart Shop
Trade hearts for your desires.

She hesitated for a moment longer before opening the door.

"Welcome. Please come this way," a male voice said from behind the counter. Cordial. With a hint of a smile. The words rolled off the tip of his tongue so naturally it was as though they were part of it.

She swallowed, her nervous pulse visible against her neck.

The door swung shut behind her.

She approached the counter.

"Good evening, esteemed client. Are you here to trade hearts?"

A trickle of sweat ran down her temple. "Y-Yes."

A piece of paper and a pen slid towards her from the other side. "Please fill in your information and state what you would like to trade for. The Heart Shop would like to inform you that all transactions are non-refundable. Please read the fair-trade policies down at the bottom of the page before you sign."

The young lady reached for the pen. The next moments of silence were broken by the tip of the pen scratching paper.

She reached the bottom.

It is hereby agreed that:

1. *The Heart Shop will decide the value of each Desire and redeem appropriate payment from the client.*
2. *Once the Desire is granted, the Trade is deemed successful and the Client shall pay the price of the Trade as agreed in the clause above.*
3. *The Client shall be solely responsible for the effect of the Trade. The Heart Shop shall bear no responsibility for any losses or liabilities as a result of the Trade.*
4. *All transactions are non-refundable.*

Her hand paused over the signature line. She opened her mouth to ask a question. The words were stuck at the back of her throat. She could barely see the person behind the counter.

"Do you require any assistance, esteemed client?"

Her voice shook a little. "Am I allowed to trade for anything?"

"Yes, of course. The Heart Shop strives to fulfil every client's wish. Please bear in mind, however, each Desire is of different weight and value based on its relative importance in the esteemed client's heart."

The young lady signed the paper and handed it over.

"Thank you. Please wait a moment."

There was silence as he read the form.

The young lady swallowed. "Will my wish be granted?"

In a voice as soft as a flickering candle, he asked in return, "What are you willing to trade?"

Another trickle of sweat. "Everything."

Behind the counter, the ends of his lips lifted slowly. He smiled like a child who had been presented with his favorite candy. "Would you like to see for yourself?"

Chapter One

Elsewhere, a man turned on the lights in his bedroom.

The wallpapers were peeling off, revealing walls the color of used oil. A half-made queen bed stood at one corner with sheets sliding off the edge, flanked by a sturdy nightstand and a medium-sized wardrobe. A dresser topped with a mirror faced the door, a set of cosmetics belonging to his wife seated on the scratched surface.

Yesterday's newspaper lay open on the floor by the foot of the bed. The headline read, "Sixteen Missing People in a Month – Council Found Remains, Strongly Hinted at the Involvement of the Otherworldly."

He caught sight of himself in the mirror and frowned at his reflection. His shirt was rumpled, as though he had just taken it out from the wash and forgot to iron it before putting it on. He hardly drank, but he looked like a depressed second-rate who spent all his time chugging shots at the pub down the street.

With a weary sigh, he started to unbutton his shirt. Halfway through, his fingers stopped. He stared hard at the button. White with a golden tinge in the middle tainted with a streak of blood.

For a moment, he was puzzled. Why did he feel like he had done this many times before?

His phone rang. Out of instinct, he reached for it.

The screen was lit but blank.

A frown creased his forehead. *Doesn't this happen every night...?*

Something was stirring inside him, trying to get out.

Remember.

Or not.

His eyes darted around -

And froze.

His reflection stared back at him from the mirror.

But it was not him - his skin was pallid and wrinkled, his eyes sunken.

He watched with growing horror as the reflection shifted. His face elongated, every bone prominent, and his eyes retracted into his skull, leaving behind empty hollows.

With a yell, he fell backward, clutching his face, nearly tripping over the stool behind him in the process.

The face in the mirror smiled a crooked smile. It opened its mouth and said, "Thank you, Master."

He let out a scream, pointing at the mirror. "W-Who are you?"

"That's the thing you've been raising inside you."

He flipped around, eyes round with terror.

Leaning against the wall next to the door, her arms crossed, was a girl he had not noticed earlier.

In a hoarse voice, he directed the same question at her: "Who are you?"

She did not answer. Instead, her lips parted in a half-sigh.

He scrutinized her with suspicion, wondering if she was a hallucination or someone who had brazenly broken into his house.

A teenage girl – no older than his wife when he first met her. She wore a black coat over her school uniform, complete with a loose tie around her neck and a pair of boots. The ends of her red hair barely touched her shoulders. Beneath the hood was a pair of unfaltering hazel eyes.

He tried his best to hold his voice steady. "My wife will be home soon. Get out before I call the cops."

"You can't. There's no police here. Even if there is, don't you think you should be more worried about yourself?"

The world flickered.

He drew himself into a defensive stance. "S-Stop spouting nonsense." He picked up his phone and shook it in front of her in an attempt to intimidate her. "Look, I'm really going to call-"

He caught sight of the blank screen and faltered.

"Mr. Panell, in this Territory, the only things that exist are you, me, and the thing you raised."

"I...you...what are you talking about? I'm telling you to get out of my house! I need to prepare dinner. My wife is coming home soon.

Another flicker – this time stronger

"No one is coming home."

"Stop spewing nonsense! I'm not having an intruder come into *my* house and -"

"Then, what is that?" The girl gestured at the cabinet.

On the topmost rack sat a memorial plate with a picture of a smiling lady. Below it was written, *In loving memory of Marylin.*

There was a clatter as Panell dropped his phone.

*

He ran down the streets towards the hospital, the rain blinding his eyes, but he did not care.

The figure beneath the covers were familiar.

"Mr. Panell, I'm sorry to break this news to you. We suspect it was a hit-and-run. We're tracking down the culprit, but your wife...I'm sorry."

Her face was as white as sheet, eyes closed in peaceful slumber, unable to hear his sobs.

How he cried and begged the gods, but none responded to him. What was the use of an apology? He would never see her again. The fact stabbed his heart like icicles.

*

A Pulse. A glimpse of his memories.

A Seed, sprouting from the Master's wishes, nourished by anguish and regret, dug deep into its Master's memories and created a space of illusions to fulfil their desires. This space was the Seed's home, its playground. It was the commander of an army, the leader of a pack of wolves, the host of a banquet.

It made the rules. Everything worked according to its whims.

It could gift the Master the most beautiful dream he ever had. It could also beget the worst nightmare that would leave the boldest of man in crippling despair.

In a Territory, logic and common sense played no role.

Everything was interconnected, down to the last strand of the Master's emotions. His memories and emotions became part of hers. She felt his helpless, suffocating sorrow.

The only difference was that he was the Master, and she was the Hunter, and a Hunter knew how to differentiate emotions that did not belong to them.

It did not, however, eliminate the fact that she could still feel what he felt.

"No! Lies! All lies! She is not dead!" Panell swept the contents off the dresser. The jars of cosmetics smashed onto the floor, spilling their contents everywhere.

"I'll give you a chance to see your wife again. Would you take it?"

A figure in a black robe held out a hairpin decorated with an inky gem. The hairpin reminded him of the gift he gave her during their first date.

A chance to see her again. Hadn't he asked himself the same question over and over?

If only he was on time that day...

If only she didn't wait for him...

If only he could turn back time...

If only...

Even if he had to pay with his life, he would accept it without hesitation.

Rin opened her eyes.

Panell was hunched over, sobbing. "Lies... All of these...lies..."

Black aura was leaking out of him like spires, twirling around him.

Seeds, by nature – sly, cunning, and calculative – thrived on strong emotions, diving deep into their Master's hearts, preying on their desires and feeding on them, twisting their minds and leading them to do its bidding.

"How many people have you fed to it? You turned yourself into a murderer to raise it, but a Seed would never repay its Master in the way you wanted it to."

"You're wrong. She is at work. She will come back soon, like she did every day." He jabbed a finger at her. "You're lying!"

He looked towards where the door was, expecting his wife to step through it..

There was no door.

His face crumpled as reality sank in.

As they fed, Seeds gave the Master what they wanted most in return – the Master's memories serving as fundamentals to build a Territory that provided moments of ephemeral bliss.

He looked up, his eyes wild and dark. "I just need to... One person...then I will see her again."

Stretching out his hand, he took one step towards her, then another.

"Give... Would you give me your life?" His head and neck shuddered unnaturally.

"Did you ask everyone you killed?"

He looked down at himself and then back at her in a daze. "What do you mean? I just want..." Holding out his hands like a desperate beggar, he implored, "Give...Give it to me."

The Seed had slowly taken over its Master's mind without him realizing it, corrupting his heart and using his twisted conscience as a catalyst for the final stages of its growth.

His knees buckled into strange angles. With a burst of energy, he careened towards her like a giant toddler. *"Give me your life!"*

Rin sidestepped him and lashed out with a kick to his jaw, sending him flying across the room. "Come and get it then."

"It's unfair. It's unfair! I just want to see her again. What's wrong with that?" Laughter bubbled up from between his sobs. "I just... I just... I just..."

He sounded like malfunctioning clockwork.

She let out a short, incredulous laugh. "How are you planning to face your wife with so much blood on your hands?"

At an earlier stage, this Seed presented its Master with a blissful Territory. When the Seeds had eaten their fill and gained enough to mature, they would withdraw the gift. Unable to withstand the shock, the already-fragile Master's mind would collapse, and the Seed would consume the Master whole.

At this point, the Master was beyond saving. Rin had known that even before arriving.

For the past month, there had been news of people going missing in the vicinity. By the time the Council found the source – a middle-aged man who lost his wife three years ago and was never able to come to terms with it, the area was dense with Seed miasma.

At the rate it grew, it was clear how well the Master fed it.

There was only one thing left to do.

A blade appeared in her hand.

Panell picked himself up, muttering the same words over and over to himself, shaking.

Pointing the blade at him, she ordered, "Show yourself!"

The Master's eyes rolled backward. He shuddered violently from head to toe. His back arched, and the muscles at his neck strained. A gurgling sound emerged from his throat.

Blackish, wet, slimy shapes appeared at the edge of his open mouth - fingers.

Then, a rounded shape pushed its way through – the head, followed by the neck and then its shoulders.

Everything about it looked like a freak sculpture gone wrong.

Its three faces were grotesque masks. The exposed skin was wrinkled like a century-old tree, and its arms were inhumanely long. Its fingers dripped ichor.

The creature was forcing its way out of its Master's mouth like a butterfly emerging from its cocoon for the first time.

Except that this was a hideous transformation.

Sensing its predator, the Seed turned its beady eyes toward her.

Choking sounds came from his throat as he tried to speak. His eyes darted back and forth between her and the Seed.

She knew better than to question if this was the ending the Master deserved. He might have been under the influence of the Seed when he killed dozens in cold blood and fed the victims to it. Some might say it was his karma, but in the end, it all boiled down to one conclusion: he gave himself to the Seed's temptation and paved the way to becoming an empty husk to accommodate the parasite.

Perhaps if they had detected the source earlier...perhaps he could be saved.

But pondering over *perhaps* was pointless at this stage. By the law of the world, Seeds were abominations that shouldn't exist. They were not allowed to live among humans. Hence, it became a Hunter's responsibility to destroy them.

Ironic, because Seeds grow from the hearts of humans.

"H-Help," Panell managed to rasp.

When the Seed became one with the Master, killing the Seed also meant killing the Master.

Black tendrils erupted from the Seed and shot towards her. She sidestepped them as several of them plunged into the floorboards, narrowly missing her feet. Conjuring blue flames that engulfed the rest of the tendrils, she closed the distance between her and the Seed in the blink of an eye, blade drawn.

A Seed in the process of assimilating itself with its host was at its weakest, unable to move before its host completely succumbed to its control.

She caught a glimpse of the Master's face – empty, soulless eyes with dried streaks of tears down his cheeks. Perhaps releasing him from this hell was also an act of mercy.

There was a flash of silver followed by a loud shriek as the Seed was ripped into two Collapsing into itself, it shattered into millions of pieces. Sparkling debris floated down like snow over what remained of the Master.

Panell's body crumpled to the floor.

The Territory vanished, and she found herself at its entry point: the doorstep of Panell's house. The lights were off, and any trace of life inside had disappeared along with the Seed's presence.

She did not bother going in to check. Instead, she turned and left.

It had started to rain, droplet after droplet falling faster and larger, like splatters of paint over the asphalt.

Rin Elziel let out a long sigh and closed her eyes. The late autumn wind whipped past her, playfully snagging her hair and biting her skin through the coat.

She found no sense of accomplishment from this assignment. In the three years she had been a Hunter, how many times had she seen Masters driving themselves to the point of no return? How many hearts and memories of such Masters had she seen? At some point, she stopped asking herself what depth of desperation made them go to such lengths. After all, dying in the hands of a Seed would not accomplish anything.

It was human nature to give in to temptations. Desires were very powerful weaknesses.

She remembered the Master's empty eyes, staring into infinity, yet unseeing.

For a brief moment, she realized how her back felt. Cold. With a hint of vulnerability.

Then, like water sliding off a gutter, the feeling disappeared. The assignment was over, as it should be.

She drew her hood back over her head and stepped out into the rain.

CHAPTER TWO

The older side of Creave was the epitome of disorganized beauty. Narrow cobblestone streets and uneven steps wound around brick houses and shops that claimed their spots wherever they liked, yet managed to fit together like a perfect puzzle. A stretch of clear sky was visible between red roofs. A canal ran through the center of town, sporting riverside merchants on boats. Blossom trees lined the waterside. In a few months' time, the ground would be covered in a carpet of petals. Somewhere around the corner, a bard regaled the afternoon with his flute. The sound of flowing water, the rustle of leaves, and the peaceful hustle of the townsfolk blended like a seamless, harmonious melody.

The magic woven within the lands of Ilias threaded themselves in every fiber of Creave, rolling through the town and across its countryside, manifesting as unrestrained meadows and wildflowers, and ending in lush hills. It ran through the blood of the people, thriving with diversity, manifesting naturally through their fingertips.

Rin inhaled the familiar scent of Creave: fresh apples, roasted chestnuts, freshly-baked bread. She felt at home, like she had known the place all her life just like the warm patchwork blanket her grandmother had made for her when she was a child.

When she first set foot here three years ago, it had been a breezy afternoon on a late spring day. The vast countryside greeted her with a dozen colors. Sunlight drenched the meadows and wildflowers bobbed in the wind, flashing their gold petals among the bright green blades of grass. The rustling of the leaves, the gurgling of water from the nearby brook, birds chirping loud and clear –

Everything had sparkled. Welcoming her.

At that moment, she felt that everything was alive. Not because of magic, but because it just was.

*

Shortbread Factory was a unique building, previously an old studio with a loft and remodeled into a living space. Its name had been coined by Edwin over tea on a random afternoon – to Mirelle's delight and Cnaris' disapproval.

The dining room was filled with the comforting scent of roasted chicken pie Mirelle made for dinner. Two people glowered at each other over a pot of mushroom soup on the table.

"I am not taking any extra classes," Rin said, enunciating each word.

"Tell that to your father." Cnaris lifted his cup of tea and sniffed, appreciating the aroma.

"How about telling him to mind his own business?"

"How about going along with what he says for once?"

Rin's mentor and landlord, Cnaris Salinas, was a man in his early thirties. He was once a professional assassin, before he decided to quit and start working for the Council for reasons he refused to reveal, and Rin had no interest in finding out.

He lived on blunt sarcasm and had a pure hate relationship with dirt and untidiness, so he was forever clean-shaven and wore clothes that had been ironed. He had only two kinds of expressions, differentiated by a small frown. One was his usual poker face; another was when he discovered a giant bag of dust bunnies hiding at the back of his kitchen cupboard.

Rin inhaled, trying to remain as calm as she could. "Why does he think I need extra classes? I'm doing fine!"

"He thinks you've been going on too many assignments and falling behind in studies," Cnaris said in a flat tone that matched his expression. "I think he got a hold of your lackluster midterms."

Unbelievable. "That was just once -" She clenched her fists, red rising in her face, realizing how childish she sounded. "What makes him think he can make decisions for me?"

When he hasn't given a damn about his daughter for years.

"He said if you object, you should inform him of your reasons personally," Cnaris said, still wearing the same bored expression. "I'm done becoming his mouthpiece."

Comprehension dawned on Rin. "Oh, so he just wanted me to show up." She slammed her hands on the table. The glassware rattled. "I'm not going!"

 Cnaris tutted. "If they break, I'll deduct the damage from your pay – plus interest."

"All right, all right, let's all settle down." Mirelle came out of the kitchen and set the freshly baked chicken pie in front of them. Serving slices on plates, she said, "Why don't you give Rin a break?"

Mirelle, housekeeper and peacemaker, proudly accepted her role as the motherly figure who watched Rin grow through her rebellious teenage years. She was the only other inhabitant of the factory warehouse that Cnaris claimed as his house and office, and was undeniably the biggest contributor to the household. She could clean the dirtiest of rooms with a wave of hand, but she preferred manual labor. Magic was meant to facilitate, not to make people lazy.

Sparkling glassware, spotless furniture, timely meals, hot tea, and the best shortbread in town. Without her, Cnaris and Rin would be living like beggars, like how it had been before they met her. Most importantly, her words broke fights between the two hotheads eighty percent of the time. Ten percent of the time, she was indifferent. The other ten percent involved Rin's father.

"I'm not going anywhere tonight or the night after," Rin declared. "The assignment was tiring; I need rest."

"You don't have a say in this. After all, you're just a freeloader."

"You take part of my wages for each assignment," Rin said, appalled.

"Yeah." Cnaris rolled his eyes. "As if that's enough to raise a stubborn mule and deal with her father, who calls every other day. Don't you think I deserve more credit?"

"Cnaris!" Mirelle admonished.

Rin set her cup down with a *thunk*.

"I knew you would object to the extra classes, so I prepared an alternative." Cnaris held up a slip of paper between his fingers.

Rin snatched it from him and opened it. Inside were the details of a new assignment due in the next twenty-four hours. She stared at it, incredulous. "Am I a slave now?"

"Rin just came back from her last assignment. Aren't you being too hard on her?" Mirelle frowned, handing out the plates.

"I think it's a perfect excuse. I do need to give your father an explanation," Cnaris said with a hint of smugness. "Tomorrow night, at that location."

Great, she thought, skimming through the words written on the paper. It sounded like a job for more than one person. Neither Kazu nor Edwin were back.

Cnaris sipped on his soup. "I'm also giving you a chance to take out your anger."

Her mentor sure loved being vague.

"Don't push yourself, Rin. If you don't want to do it, just say so." Mirelle rolled up her sleeves. "I'll fight him for it."

That made her dissent diminish ever so slightly. But she had already made up her mind.

CHAPTER THREE

Rin contemplated if skipping Thursday's afternoon classes to ride on a wobbly old bus was worth it.

She glanced at the time on her phone. Half past two. It was Math period, and she was halfway towards the town of Pallin – a good fifty minutes from Creave. She had thrown her usual black windbreaker over her school uniform, removed her tie, and left her bag in her locker. The only things she carried were some loose change, her phone, and a pair of earphones.

The bus rolled over a pothole, and every one of its loose joints began creaking in unison. Rin closed her eyes as the worn springs of her seat bounced up and down. The roaring engine drowned out the music streaming through her earphones.

The forsaken vehicle finally lurched to a stop, and she got off, thankful that she was finally on still ground. Taking out her earphones, she surveyed her surroundings. Someone had graffitied a giraffe on the walls of the bus stop. Two public phone booths with their glass sprayed stood side by side across the road. One of their doors was hanging on its hinges, victims of vandalism. Rows of shops lined the asphalt streets, with flat roofs, brick walls, and faded signs. Orderly and neat, the town exuded an air of stern history.

The traffic came to a standstill, and the pedestrian lights turned green. She crossed the road and headed straight, past the barber and a restaurant that was out of business. Two minutes later, she arrived at a three-story building that looked as though it had lived for too long and given up. Ivies owned the walls, and weeds littered the entrance. The sign above the main door had paint peeling off, and the words were barely legible.

Rin did not need to check to know that she was at the right place. The entire place reeked of a well-nourished Seed.

She ascended the dimly-lit staircase. Light filtered in through the window high up the walls, illuminating the floating dust particles. The interior fulfilled her expectations – dull corridors, cracked walls, dusty floors. Spiders made homes in corners and abandoned them. Someone's shower echoed down the corridor.

Another flight of stairs. The moment she reached the topmost step, the gray walls disappeared, replaced by an open space of warmth and sunshine. The sudden brightness hurt her eyes. When she lowered her arm, she was standing on a farm. Raised beds were filled with fresh, green crops. A small farmhouse stood a short distance away. An elderly man was watering the plants, wiping his forehead with a grimy towel draped around his neck.

"Granddad, I've gotten most of them!" A girl a few years older than Rin hurried towards the elderly man, carrying a basket of juicy, red tomatoes. "Look, aren't they lovely?"

"Yes, we got a good harvest this year. I told you we're blessed by your green fingers," Granddad said heartily. "The neighbors would be pleased."

"Aw, Granddad, these are your hard work. Aren't you sorry to see them go?"

"Sharing is always caring, my lovely granddaughter." Granddad chuckled.

This place spelled laughter and joy, smelled of earth and life, glowing like a wonderful summer vacation. Beneath it was a heavy sense of longing and sadness, and deeper than that, the hatred that built the very foundation of the land.

Territories like these sickened Rin to the core.

"They are our best produce, and good things should be shared, not kept to ourselves. Nothing makes me happier than seeing people enjoying a bowl of stew made from our hard work." He caught sight of Rin. "Oh, hello, are you Lyndia's friend?"

Rin gave her best smile. "Yes, Mr. Reily."

Lyndia's smile faded.

"It's rare for Lyndy to have a friend over," Granddad said, delighted. He gave the girl a small nudge. "Where are your manners? Bring your friend in. I'll get the tea boiling."

Rin felt Lyndia's stony silence and suspicious eyes following her into the house.

To Granddad, she was Lyndia's friend. To Lyndia, she was an intruder.

Their home was cozy and humble. The walls were decorated with handmade wreaths. Two wicker chairs sat by the windows overlooking the farm, and the cracks between the lace curtains invited in sun that created rhomboids on the parquet floor. Several photographs sat on the mantlepiece: one of Lyndia when she was a child, one of her and a young couple whose faces were strategically hidden by light reflecting off the surface – presumably her parents, whom she could probably not remember well enough – and the newest one of her and Granddad, both beaming while holding up freshly harvested radishes.

Rin ran her hand over the wooden surface of the table in the corner of the room, wonderfully rough and genuine.

The Seed had to be very well-fed to give its Master such a beautiful Territory.

"Who are you?" Lyndia stood behind her.

Instead of answering the question, Rin gestured at the first two photographs. "Did your Granddad take these?"

Lyndia steeled herself and finally walked over to get a better view. "Yes, he took them. When Mum and Dad passed, he raised me. All these years, single-handedly, on this farm."

"You didn't want to move from here."

"This land was not ours to begin with. The authorities are reclaiming it..." Her eyes narrowed. "How did you know we're moving? Who are you to begin with?"

"You loved it here," Rin said, looking at the photographs. Lyndia was either smiling or laughing in each one of them. The girl standing in front of her was an empty husk. Her eyes were bottomless pools of regret and hatred she was drowning herself in. "If you had not moved, then *that* would not have happened – is what you're thinking?"

There was a long silence.

"What do you mean?" Lyndia said, almost in a whisper.

"You two would not have had to attempt to make a living in a faraway town. You would not have met him, and your Granddad would not have died."

She was stating a fact – not eliciting a conversation.

The color drained from Lyndia's face. "Who are you?"

"The girl who Granddad doted on, where is she? All I see is a pair of eyes crazed for revenge. Is that really what you want?"

She raised her voice. "I said, *who are you?*"

"Your Granddad would be disappointed if he knew you were harboring the same thing that killed him-"

"Shut up!"

Somewhere, an uneasy, slumbering aura stirred.

"That you choose to relieve your memory of him this way-"

"Shut up!" Lyndia closed the distance between them, eyes blazing. Her voice was barely a whisper. "I will never forgive that man. Never! Granddad was always, always, *always* good and kind to everyone, even to a jerk like him, even if he treated us like garbage beneath his feet."

When they first met the boss, he looked imposing in a suit and dark glasses. Wealth. Authority. He was from a different world. She could not even look him in the eye – she felt that it would be improper to. He looked at her from top to bottom, lifted her chin so that he could see her face properly, and said in a careless tone, "What a pity, too plain-looking to attend to my guests. I suppose you'll have to work in the kitchen, then."

Working at the bistro was hard labor and not the least bit rewarding. She had to wash dozens of cutlery, run errands for the chefs, and get the stocks ready for the next day. Her superiors yelled at her for being slow, when she was trying her hardest to be fast. They shouted at her for mistakes that were not hers. Most of the time, she barely had time for meals.

Granddad's job as a cleaner and caretaker was worse than hers, being the first to arrive and the last to leave. Her heart ached to see him bending over tables to sweep up peanut shells, cigarette butts, and all sorts of junk uncivilized customers took the liberty of throwing on the floor. The pair of hands were meant to grow crops, not to clean out rubbish, but he always laughed at her woes.

"Our hands are meant to do all kinds of work, to provide for the ones we cherish. It doesn't matter what it is we are doing, as long as we can make a living. Money is hard to come by, Lyndy. We have food, clothes, and a roof over our heads – we must be grateful." He chuckled. "If you miss our old home, we can always raise a few potted plants here."

The Pulse, like all the others, was disorientating and unpleasant.

Lyndy's face was as dark as thunder. "He killed Granddad and walked free." Her eyebrows knitted together as tears glinted in her eyes. "He bribed the authorities, and they declared Granddad died because of a cardiac arrest when he was actually murdered."

A luxury car pulled up in front of her, and the window of the back passenger seat rolled down. He wore a suit that probably cost three months' rent for the apartment she was staying in, a pair of round sunglasses with golden frame, and held a smoking cigar between his fingers.

"Hey, I heard the old man's funeral is today. Got money?"

She clenched her fists. He saw it and laughed. "Oh, come on. If you need money, just say it. I am your benefactor, after all."

He took a check out of his pocket and handed it to her. "I liked him. What a pity. If only he didn't stick his nose where he shouldn't. Well, the old man worked hard all his life. I guess it's time he got proper rest." He took a drag of the cigarette and puffed out smoke in her face. The check slipped from his fingers and fell to the ground. *"Whoops."* He smirked. *"Guess you have to pick that up."*

The window rolled up, and the car drove away, leaving her standing on the side of the street. The tears that she struggled hard to contain rolled down her cheeks as black anger filled her heart.

"I swore I would be the one who gives him what he deserves."

"Tea is ready." Granddad entered with a tea tray. He hesitated by the door, sensing the tension between them.

"Is – is everything all right?" His eyes darted back and forth between Rin and Lyndia.

Lyndia hastily wiped her eyes with the back of her hand and recomposed herself. "It's fine, Granddad. We're just talking."

He blinked at them. "Lyndia grew up with only me and a few old folks as company. She might be a little spoilt, sometimes a little rough-tempered and a little sentimental, but – but she is a good girl. She has a good heart. If she offended you or did something wrong, please do not take it to heart -"

"I understand. Please don't worry," Rin said, in her politest voice.

"I – I see." His expression of uncertainty melted into a laugh. "Carry on, then. Don't let the old man bother you. After all, we're moving out the day after tomorrow – might as well make the most of it, hmm?"

Lyndia turned away so that he couldn't see her eyes glistening. "If I'd known all this earlier, Granddad, we would never have moved."

He chuckled. "What are you talking about, silly child? Where else are we going to live?"

Before he left, he looked over Lyndia's shoulder and met Rin's gaze. With a small, knowing smile, he gave her a small nod.

Rin's eyes widened.

Just now, what did he do?

The illusion broke, and they were both in a cramped, dim space that was so messy that Cnaris would have thrown a fit if he were there. The laundry basket was overflowing with dirty clothes. Unwashed plates piled in the sink and on the table. Half-eaten snack packets and cup noodles were strewn all over the floor. The bed was buried under another pile of laundry and unfolded blankets. The curtains were drawn, and the poor plants sitting by the windows were wilting due to the lack of sunlight and water. The air was heavy with the stench of sweat, mold, and Seed.

Rin glanced at the photographs on the shelves, the same as the ones in the Territory.

Seeds either grew from its Master's heart – or cultivated from a cursed Sygn. A Seed that grew purely from its Master's heart would not give its Master such a bright, blissful Territory. Neither would it grow so quickly.

Lyndia gave her a bitter smile. "Seen enough? Now, get out." She pointed at the door. "I don't even care who you are anymore. Just get out."

"Where did you get it from?"

"Why do I have to tell you?"

"Do you know what the consequences are? The price you'll have to pay?"

"Price? I don't care what price. I'd pay with my life." Lyndia walked towards Rin, her hands clutching her chest. "I don't want to live with this pain anymore. It hurt so bad that I wanted to rip my heart out. Granddad was my only family, and that beast of a man took him away from me.He admitted that in my face, in front of Granddad's body, and he said the law would not be able to touch him, that he was invincible. The investigators could not find any proof that it was murder. He gave them money, and they closed the case. I couldn't accept it. Just because he has money, he's allowed to do as he wishes? Is this a special privilege for the wealthy? Does the law only serve the rich and leave everyone else to rot on their own?

She took another step closer, her eyes hollow. "Do you know what my biggest regret was? That night, I shouldn't have listened to Granddad. He told me to leave early. If only I had been there, then maybe it wouldn't have happened. I've thought about it over and over. I thought I was going crazy. I couldn't do anything until someone granted my wish. This was my only hope. I'd willingly give it everything I had. At least, I could live with Granddad. Even if it's just an illusion, it's enough."

"Is that what you thought?" Rin said quietly.

"Was it not?"

"I don't know," Rin said. "Because the dead do not speak."

Lyndia half-laughed, half-sobbed.

"I do know one thing, though. This is not something your Granddad would want."

"Get out!" Lyndia's voice rose to a scream. For the briefest of moment, the room quaked. One of the photographs toppled over, the dirty dishes rattled, and a potted plant fell off the sill with a crash. She held up a jet-black object in the shape of a hilt. "Get out before I set it free!"

Rin grabbed her wrist and hissed, temper rising, "Set it free, then. Because I'm here to destroy it."

"You're a Hunter?" Lyndia scoffed. "I should've known."

"You're just one step away from being its food. Seeds never stop eating. No matter how much you feed them, they are forever hungry. The more you feed them, the hungrier they get, until one day, they eat their own Master. Do you think those blissful illusions of your Granddad are your salvation? They are proof that the Seed is eating your mind. That killer is a servant to richness, and you are the Seed's puppet. How different are you from him?"

"I don't care."

"You are willing to give the life your Granddad painstakingly raised with everything he had to a despicable Seed?" Rin demanded.

"You will *never* know what it felt like to lose someone you love and be unable to do anything about it!"

The words hit Rin like an iron-clad punch.

His hand, slick with blood, slid from her grasp. In the pouring rain, all that was left was his jacket. However much she refused to believe it happened, the outcome would not change.

Lyndia wrenched her hand free from Rin's loosened grasp and stormed out the door, leaving her standing in the cluttered space alone.

CHAPTER FOUR

For three hours, Rin was the only customer at the Golden Beans Café.

Three empty cups and several pieces of crumpled tissues sat on the table in front of her. The fourth was three-quarters empty. There was nothing golden about the coffee. The more she drank, the more difficult it was to stomach. She blamed her poor appetite on the heavy Seed miasma that spread outwards from the opposite bistro like a contagious disease.

The Island Club Bistro was built on privately owned land. It had a eye-catching, angular design that looked out of place in the orderly streets of Pallin. The glass windows were tinted, obscuring the interior. The outdoors had ample parking and a neatly manicured lawn decorated with fairy lights.

The cafe owner sat behind the counter, looking as colorless and bland as the coffee he made, paying no attention to his only customer of the day. On the next table, a newspaper spread draped over the edge. The small article squeezed in the corner of the page was titled "Pallin's Osmanthus St. - The Latest Hit in Town."

Osmanthus St. in Pallin has been a hit with tourists in the last few months. Sellers have reported triple the number of visitors compared to the same quarter in the last year. Famed for its vibrance and night lights, the Eastern Times *asked the public what exactly made Osmanthus St. a tourist favorite –*

There was an event of sorts going on at the bistro. At four, the staff bustled in and out, putting up flowers, tying ribbons, and rolling out the red carpet. At half past six, the sun began to set, and the fairy lights came on. At seven, a luxurious black motorcade rolled into the driveway.

She was flipping through the menu for dinner when the owner, Henry Ross, stepped out of the vehicle in a shiny purple crocodile suit that glittered in the lights, his hair carefully slicked back with just the right amount of gel. His employees in uniform scrambled out to greet him. A quick background check told Rin that he was a rising entrepreneur with multiple successful projects and investments under his belt. Numerous articles praised him for being a rare talent. His interviews pictured him as a witty, inspiring young man with an excellent temperament.

The media sure loved superfluous personalities.

Rin heard him telling off one of his staff for messy hair and berated another for an abominable stain on their vest. Then, he strode over the red carpet, leaving behind a sickening stench of Seed that spread across the street.

That man was also harboring a well-fed one.

Irritated, she slammed the menu shut and asked for another cup of coffee.

The bistro staff remained lined up at the entrance as car after car arrived, each bringing an important guest who was welcomed by an usher. Rin had minimal knowledge of luxurious car brands; all she knew was they were individually more expensive than Cnaris' renovated warehouse.

At eight, the most luxurious car – she figured, because it was the biggest so far – rolled up. The chauffeur leaped down and jogged to the other side to open the back passenger door. A man in a gray suit stepped out, surveying the vicinity. Ross came hurrying out of the bistro with a wide smile. They exchanged greetings in boisterous voices and shook hands like old friends before Ross ushered him in.

"That's the VVIP," a voice said beside her. "I heard he owns a conglomerate. You know, the luxury lagoon and casino complex in the West Coast. Mr. Ross is trying to get him to invest in his new resort project. Think he minds three people gatecrashing his party for some fine dining experience?"

Rin's eyes narrowed. She glanced to her right. Standing under the streetlamp close to where she was sitting was a pair of identical twins.

Tanned olive skin, caramel brown hair tied into a low ponytail, and yellow eyes that seemingly gleamed in the dark. The Signon twins, rival Hunters and mischief-makers. The people she least wanted to see at the moment. They were a year her junior and worked under a mentor Cnaris despised. The last time the three of them happened to work together, they wrecked the entire street, and Rin ended up with no pocket money for the rest of the month.

"What do you mean *three* people?" Rin hissed as the waiter brought her fifth cup of coffee and wordlessly left. "Why are you even here?"

Rayve, the older twin, scowled. "That's supposed to be our question. Why are *you* here? We accepted the assignment before anyone else did."

Cnaris, she growled silently in her heart. That two-faced schemer. He must be eating Mirelle's freshly made dinner without a shred of remorse.

Seeing Rin's expression, the younger, diplomatic twin tugged at his brother's sleeve. "Rayve, maybe the Council made a mistake and released the assignment on the board after we took it. It's not the first time they've done that."

Rayve rolled his eyes. "Yeah, what a coincidence. Each time it's happened, we meet her."

Whatever, Rin thought. She just wanted to get it over with and go home.

"We saw you this afternoon – when you went after the Master," Hayle chipped in brightly. "You could've destroyed the Seed. Why didn't you?"

"Do you think destroying the Seed will solve everything?"

Hayle cocked his head. He reminded Rin of a cockatiel. "Isn't that what the orders are?"

He was partly right. That was what the orders were – to destroy the Seeds. Rin could have wrenched the Sygn from the girl and destroyed it there and then. Or she could have evoked enough fury from the Master within the Territory and forced the Seed to appear.

But the Council's orders left out an important factor: the human heart. The two years away from Creave with Cnaris, she had seen plenty, enough to know human hearts were not something as superficial as orders could suppress.

Desires. Regrets. Sorrow. Emotions ran deep and rampant, weaving themselves within the deepest crevices of the heart and obscuring any form of logic and rationale.

Hayle was expecting an answer from her, his eyes bright and earnest.

She heaved a sigh and forced herself to elaborate. "Destroying the Seed would not uproot the source that led to its manifestation in the first place. For as long as they carry the grudge, they will fall into the same pothole again and again. Figure it out yourselves."

Comprehension dawned on Hayle's face as he digested her words and he opened his mouth to answer.

Rayve cut in. "Enough with the talking. Fine, we'll split this. You'll go after the girl; we'll go after that man." He jerked his head towards the bistro.

Impatient as always, she thought. Out loud, she said, "Just so you know, I'm not up for any of your trickery tonight."

"Aw, don't be like that. We're going to work together this time. Can we set our grudges – if there are any – aside?" Hayle said, pulling up a chair and sitting down next to her.

Both Rin and Rayve stared at him.

He beamed at them both. "So, what's the plan?"

*

The aromas of a feast wafted out through the open kitchen windows and teased her nostrils. Her empty stomach rumbled in protest.

Her brother taught her that instincts were the most trustworthy ally in the most unexpected times. Right then, Rin had serious doubts about her instincts. The last-minute plan involved her standing alone in the back alley, next to bags of leftovers, trying not to think about food. The drain belched out dishwater now and then. Loud music blasted from speakers, the beats changing according to the whims of the DJ. Occasional bursts of raucous laughter and chinks of glassware came through the windows.

Just when she thought her patience was reaching its limit, she saw a figure approaching the back door.

It turned out Rei was right – instincts were trustworthy.

Under the cap that hid half her face, Lyndia's eyes held a murderous glint. She pushed the back door open, and golden light poured out. Before she could enter, Rin emerged from the shadows, grabbed her by the coat, and dragged her into the alley.

"You!" Lyndia accused.

Rin gestured at her to be quiet. The door swung wide, and a bag of kitchen waste flew out, landing next to the pile that was already there, before slamming shut.

Lyndia shook herself free from Rin and snarled, "I'm warning you, do not try to interfere."

"You're really stubborn, aren't you? Doing harm to another person is not as easy as you think."

Lyndia's lips curved into a sneer. "I've been waiting for this day."

She turned and headed for the door.

Trust your instincts.

"How about a gamble?" Rin offered. "If you manage to commit the crime without hesitation, I will not interfere. When you become part of the Seed, I'll destroy you just like how I would the other Seeds."

Lyndia stopped and turned around, her expression unfathomable.

"But if you show a single moment of hesitation, I will destroy that thing in front of your eyes."

"Why do I need to listen to what you say?"

"Because if you don't" – a knife appeared in Rin's hand – "I'll destroy it right here and now. You know you're no match for me. I'm giving you a chance."

Trust your instincts.

The other girl's expression hardened. A moment later, she squared her shoulders and set her jaw. "Just don't get in my way."

She did not look back.

Rin gave her a five-second head start before following.

The bistro was larger than it looked from the outside. The corridor connecting the kitchen and the guest area was a narrow one. The floor trembled with the booming bass, accentuated by techno beats.

Lyndia strode through the corridor as though she owned the place. Waiters squeezed past, refilling trays and shouting hurried orders at each other, not sparing the two of them a glance.

She pushed past a set of heavy black curtains, emerging in a whole new world. The cramped corridor opened into a lounge. Scantily clad performers spun around with elaborate moves, egging the crowd to join. Colorful lights spun over the dance floor at a dizzying pace. The rest of the lighting was dramatically dimmed so that the people looked like silhouettes, dark enough to hide faces, but not enough to bump into each other. Bartenders stood behind the counter, shaking up cocktails and pouring shots, impressing ladies with their skills. The sweet scent of alcohol went well with the mouth-watering smell of newly smoked turkey. Waiters walked around serving champagne, unlike their frantic compatriots behind the scenes. The tables were occupied with talks of potential investments, casual pleasantries, and gossip over huddled heads.

At the center of the lounge, in a black leather sofa with ladies hanging onto each arm, was Henry Ross. He was engaged in deep conversation with his very important guest, who dabbed his mouth with a napkin and nodded approvingly.

Lyndia took a cocktail from the counter and made her way up the stairway opposite the lounge. At the landing hung another curtain presumably concealing Ross' gift to his honored guest, which he would reveal at the climax of the event.

Henry Ross and his guest stood up, shaking hands – a gesture of triumph. Whatever it was, it was clear that the deal had gone through.

Lyndia's eyes fixed on Ross the entire time, burning with hatred. Rin stopped halfway up the stairs, watching as Lyndia's hand drifted almost casually into her coat while sipping her cocktail.

The two men lifted their glasses to make a toast. The music changed to a grand tune, heralding an important announcement. The lighting shifted into indigo hues, spinning and reflecting off the walls.

Ross's voice rang out, speaking through a microphone. "Attention, ladies and gentlemen. I would like to share great news with all who have come to grace my humble establishment."

Lyndia held her Sygn in front of her. There was a flash of light as the Seed materialized, perfectly mingling with Ross's choice of lighting.

It was the biggest bee and the smallest Seed Rin had ever seen – the size of a mere three wine bottles. Two pairs of beady black eyes rimmed with gold, glossed over the surroundings and identifying its target. Its glossy, translucent wings with brown outlines vibrated on its back. It looked unassuming apart from the deadly stinger that dripped black ichor.

"The Henry Cooperation has reached an agreement with the Golden West Cooperation on the Vacation Project –"

No one below realized what was going on.

"The project is expected to be launched next month over the beaches of the Southern Coast and consists of a luxurious resort, family-oriented theme park, restaurant chains, and spas –"

Rin felt like she was watching a stage play, one she was standing by to interrupt.

Trust your instincts.

The bee's uncanny buzzing sounded like a distant metal fan, drowning the sound of the music.

Distracted, the people below began to look for the source of the sound. Henry Ross was unaware, still keenly announcing the details of his project.

"The Vacation Project is foreseen to bring great change to the landscape of Southern Ilias, and you, dear investors, stand to reap the most from this. Let's raise our glasses to –"

One of the paid performers was the first to notice the enormous bee. With a small cry, she stumbled and fell backward.

Henry Ross' initial frown was replaced with wide-eyed shock when he saw the Seed with its stinger pointed right at him. It morphed into anger when he saw Lyndia on the landing.

"Hello, Mr. Ross. Do you remember me?" Her voice brimmed with contempt.

"Who let you in? Guards, get her!"

Bodyguards stationed at the sides of the lounge hurried towards the stairs.

Unperturbed, Lyndia raised her glass. "A toast to you, Mr. Ross."

The bee's eyes glinted with a hint of murder. The guest placed a hand on Ross' arm as the latter faltered.

"A farewell toast." Lyndia raised the glass to her lips.

The bee lunged forward.

Down below, people screamed. A few ducked beneath tables. Everyone waited with bated breath.

Except that the expected did not happen.

The bee froze mid-air.

So was Lyndia, wearing a shell-shocked expression, looking straight ahead.

"Granddad," she said in a hushed voice. The glass slipped from her fingers and crashed onto the floor. Tears started to roll down her face. "No."

The figure of her grandfather – a mirage – stood in front of her. "Don't do it, Lyndy. Don't sacrifice your life for him."

Affected by her shaken resolve, the space rippled. Rin found herself drawn into a Pulse.

*

She ran as fast as she could, dread filling her heart with every beat.

The door was open, but there were no lights. The moment she stepped into the bistro, time seemed to stop.

Her mind was unable to register the sight as a whole. Reality was a broken lie, a fragmented nightmare. Terrifying to look at, but unable to look away.

Her grandfather crumpled in a pool of his blood.

Henry Ross stood over him with a cold look on his face. Looming behind him was a fiendish creature that she could not find the words to describe. Its ragged breaths fogged the air in front of it, and blood dripped from its claws.

Granddad's blood.

She remembered screaming Granddad's name and dropping to her knees next to him. She barely remembered the flashing red lights and wailing sirens that tore the night apart.

All she remembered was holding his hand, praying that she could feel a flicker of movement.

She never did.

Lyndia shook her head, clamping her hands over her ears. "No, don't stop me. He's the one who killed you."

"Please, Lyndy, don't do it. It pains me to see you like this-"

Sorrow wracked her body as she sobbed onto Granddad's cold, motionless body. The wounds she saw earlier were gone.

No one believed her.

"The old man had a heart attack, poor thing. I called the ambulance as fast as I could, but he couldn't make it."

Lies.

"You killed him."

He gazed at her, emotionless. Then, he broke into a smile.

"Do you have evidence? Who do you think they'll believe? You or me? It takes little effort to have the police agree that it was cardiac arrest and close the case." He leaned in closer to her and said softly, "And even if they have suspicions, they can't do anything. Do you want to know why?"

Behind him, a large shadow loomed. His eyes were full of cold humor. This was child's play for him.

"Because they have no proof."

*

"He is the one who took you away from me!" Lyndia screamed. "How could I live and do nothing?"

The bee drew back, ready to plunge.

Ross scrambled back, nearly tripping over his expensive leather sofa. "Guards!"

Two of his bodyguards positioned themselves in front of him while the rest began running up the stairs.

A knife cut through the air, piercing the Seed's hard armor and impaling it onto the wall where it thrashed.

The rod suspending the curtains overhead snapped in two, and the heavy fabric fell with a *whoosh*, revealing a congratulatory message Ross had prepared in advance for the collaboration against the background of his ideal resort.

In a flash, Rin leaped over the balustrade, a slender sword appearing in her hand. She drove the blade into the Seed's body. With a shrill cry, it shattered into debris that vanished into thin air, leaving behind her throwing knife.

“No!” Lyndia cried in despair, falling to her knees.

Rin picked the knife up from the ground and turned. “You hesitated. You lost.”

CHAPTER FIVE

Turmoil tore through the bistro. People screamed and ran, tripping over each other, rushing for the exit. Ross' important guest was pale with fright, sandwiched between his guards and the shoving crowd.

Ross, on the other hand, was beside himself with fury; the distinguished demeanor of the young, successful entrepreneur had vanished. "How did a bug get in here? What is security doing?"

His security personnel, all dressed in similar suits and ties, rushed up the stairs, resembling clones of each other. Two of them restrained the crestfallen Lyndia, who made no attempt to struggle. The rest of them surrounded Rin.

"Drop your weapon," one of them said. There was an edge of uncertainty in his voice.

Rin stowed her throwing knife away without a word. The sword vanished into a red stone on her charm bracelet.

Ross turned to his guest, rubbed his hands together, and said, "Apologies, Mr. Simson. She was my former employee, a little unstable in the head, so I stopped her from coming. I suppose she was displeased with my decision."

The guest dusted his suit and squared his shoulders. "I think our collaboration should be put on hold for now. I shall take my leave."

"Please, wait a moment. I'm sure it's a misunderstanding," Ross said, grabbing Simson's arm. His words ran over each other. His eyes went in and out of focus. "I can explain."

The guest looked him up and down and brushed his hand away. "Perhaps you should find an explanation as to why you're acting odd right now."

Everyone was staring at them.

Ross laughed, stopped, and laughed again while staggering. "I-I don't know what you're talking about, Mr. Simson."

His guest threw him a look of distaste and headed for the exit with his guards on his tail.

"I'm so close, so close," His voice grew louder with every syllable. "So close. So close!"

There was a flash of movement.

A huge claw ripped through the air, slicing Simson's guard at the rear into two.

Blood splattered over the tables and walls.

Dead silence. The guard's body fell onto the floor with a thud, the remains barely recognizable.

A dark miasma clouded Ross, visible to every pair of eyes under the roof. Looming above him was the faint outline of a hideous creature, unmistakably -

"A Seed!" someone shrilled. "Mr. Ross has a Seed!"

All hell broke loose as everyone ran, tripping over feet and edges of carpets, falling over each other as they made a frantic dash for the exit.

Ross' personnel released Lyndia and scrambled for their lives.

Disbelief painted Ross' face as people dashed past him. Tables were shoved aside, chairs turned upside-down, and wall decorations ripped into ribbons.

Simson was white with fear, his voice a pitch higher than usual. "Help! S-Someone, call the Hunters!"

At the mention of Hunters, Ross turned a sickly shade of gray. A look of realization dawned on him. He could not let any witness leave alive.

The doors swung inwards, barricading the fleeing guests within the hellish walls of its Territory.

"N-no one is leaving," he stammered out.

A long arm swiped at the escaping guests. There were screams as the claw ripped through a table as easily as cutting paper. Simson's other guard, out of loyal instinct, attempted to protect his employer with shield magic, but it broke like fragile sticks. Another claw came down and swatted him aside, sending him crashing head-first into the front glass door where he lay motionless.

"You shall not leave tonight." Ross laughed at his guests. Fear crossed his face. "N-No, I... That is not what I meant. That thing –" He pointed a shaky finger at the Seed. "It's controlling me."

"Y-You're out of your mind!" Simson cried. Cold sweat beaded his forehead, his terrified eyes darting between Ross and the Seed. "I-I would never have agreed to collaborate with a Master!"

The Seed raised one of its claws and brought it down towards the stricken man.

A flash of silver shot towards the Seed , lobbing the claw off and lodging itself firmly in the opposite wall.

It took Rin a moment to realize it was a carving knife with remnants of oil visible on its blade.

Among the frenzied crowd, she saw Rayve lowering his hand.

"Who are you?" a lady huddled in the corner, her dress in tatters, whispered shakily.

The doors swung open, and Rin saw a hand waving from the entrance. Hayle's voice floated above the din. "Everyone, please keep calm and follow me. Worry not, we will ensure your safety."

"Hunters! They're here!" someone cried.

Late, Rin thought to herself. They were all already inside the Seed's Territory.

Ross looked ill, a myriad of emotions cruising across his face.

The head of the Ross household eyed him in disgust. "The Ross House does not need an underhanded successor who resorts to blackmail, bribery, and assault to carry on its name. Not once, not twice. You manage to get away because the inspector and I are acquainted, because I had to beg him to overlook your crimes. I told you to behave, yet you got carried away."

He was merely doing it to achieve his goal.

"Do you know what you did cost a life?"

The son of the rival company? He asked for it, so he paid the price.

"You brought dishonor to me and sullied the family name. You are a disgrace."

The words struck him like a discordant chord.

Disgrace? His father had never said a good word about him. Among his three sons, he was last in the line of his father's favor to inherit the family business.

"Leave while I still consider you my blood, before I turn you over to the authorities. Do not let me see your face again."

Behind his father's back, he smiled with disdain.

Do you think, Father, you're stripping me of everything? *he thought.* I will surely rise again. And I will make everyone pay for looking down on me.

"Destroy!" Ross flung his arms out in frenzy. "Destroy them all! Everyone who stands in my way!"

With a scream, he hunched over. His back bulged, and a huge claw tore through his coat fabric, sending glittering beads flying all over the floor. Then another claw came, followed by the head.

He writhed as the Seed forced itself out of him. It was enormous, reaching the ceiling. Three pairs of feet, a pair of claws, and a pair of jaws with rows of jagged teeth. From Rin's perspective, it looked like a mutated mantis that accidentally absorbed genes from the primitive ages and had them transmuted incorrectly. Its eyes surveyed the remaining guests, blinking in unison.

It let out a high-pitched cry and raised one of its claws towards the ceiling – like a giant scythe poised to swing.

Rayve dashed towards the Seed, vaulted over a table, and onto a loose ceiling beam and dropped downwards onto the Seed, one hand outstretched. His palm hovered above the Seed's head, not quite touching the surface. The air rippled with an invisible force.

As he landed on the other side of the lounge, his ability activated. The twins could create and manipulate magnetic fields. What Rayve did was create a magnetic field with the Seed at the center. Switching polarities created either a repelling or attractive force. Both, from Rin's experience, were equally destructive.

The force reverberated from within the Seed, tearing it on the inside and sending chairs and tables hurtling over the heads of the escaping guests and crashing into the walls.

What a disruptive ability.

Rin had a foreboding sense that Cnaris would make her forfeit her pocket money once again.

Grabbing a distraught Lyndia, who had lost all will to move, she dragged the girl to a safer spot behind the stairs.

The Seed let out a resounding war cry that rocked the walls. Rayve, who was about to charge forward again, was pushed back.

The Signon twins' abilities were destructive, but it had one glaring catch: they had to be in close proximity to the Seed to make it work.

The Seed began regenerating, filling its hollow middle at a rapid pace. The bistro was now a sorry sight - shattered glass, doors blown off, beams that were on the verge of giving in, and roof about to cave in.

A gale of laughter came from the center of the rubble. Shoulders shaking with mirth, his eyes carrying a crazed glow, Ross screamed, "Yes! Destroy them all! Everyone who stands in my way!"

Fully regenerated, the Seed turned its eyes on him.

"Destroy everything, just like you did before! Get rid of all evidence, all those pests! I am untouchable!"

The Seed leaned down and reached out a claw.

Ross' laughter ceased. "What? What are you doing? I told you to destroy them all!"

The claw wrapped around him, almost lovingly. Ross' feet lifted from the ground.

The Seed opened its mouth, revealing its many, many rows of jagged teeth.

Wealth and power.

With those, he could do anything.

With those, he would own the world.

Since a young age, he always had a knack for deals and agreements. Investments, black market, illegal trades, double earnings. Bungalows, resorts, and stocks. So many businesses he gained under his belt, so far ahead of his brothers. People looked up to him and praised him. So young, yet so talented.

Except for his father.

See, Father? I told you I would rise.

His businesses were major successes. He owned half the town.

Accumulating wealth became an addiction. Not enough, he wanted more.

"Traitor!" He looked down at the twitching body at his feet. He looked down and saw himself holding a bloodstained knife. His anger began to ebb, replaced by a rising tide of panic.

He dropped the weapon.

He had killed someone.

If the police found out about this, he was done for.

His estranged father would not bail him out this time.

Dispose. Dispose of the evidence quickly! His hand shook as he reached down to pick up the knife.

"It's no good, young man. They'll find evidence everywhere."

He spun around. Behind him, he saw a figure. It was too dark to make out the face.

He thought to himself, Eyewitness... There must not be any eyewitness.

"I heard you're already on the suspect list of the latest drug-smuggling circle, and they are gathering evidence as we speak. It won't be long before they arrive at your doorstep."

His hand shook. Kill him...and he'll be silent.

The voice was suddenly in his ear. "Then, you'll lose everything."

He froze. Lose everything? No, that couldn't happen!

"There has to be something... Something," he rasped.

The figure held out a piece of folded paper between his long, slender fingers. "I believe you'll need this."

"Stop! What are you doing?" Ross squirmed within the Seed's grip.

Rin ducked as the carving knife dislodged itself from the wall and zoomed toward the Seed. Another round of invisible force dragged the rest of the debris and tattered furniture toward the Seed in an attempt to crush it.

Hayle had taken the chance to approach the Seed, changing the polarities when it had its back turned and was now standing at the door with his hands clasped together.

"Hayle!" Rayve's angry voice cut over the din. "I told you to stay out of it!"

"Sorry," Hayle said sheepishly, coughing in the dust. "I can't bear to be left out of the fun, you know."

Rayve's red face and mutinous eyes were obscured by the Seed rearing its ugly head from the rubble.

The sickening sound of flesh being pierced, the steady dripping of blood, the victims' screams and gasps as life seeped out of them.

Sneaking up on them in the backstreets, blackmailing them with a letter of threat to their family, secretly dropping poison into an unsuspecting cup of coffee -

One, two, three, four, next, next, another, and another, he lost count –

In a flash, everything disappeared.

Families gathered together, weeping.

A widow collapsed on the floor from sorrow.

Turning up to pay respects in his creaseless black suit. "So sorry for your loss. He was a great friend of mine."

Handing them a check. "This is the least I can do. I hope he'll be at peace."

Accepting the tearful words of gratitude and leaving with praises in his wake. "What a wonderful person. Such kindness, such humility."

Such fools.

He was invincible. He was destined for greatness.

Flesh, blood, life. Oh, what did they matter to him?

In a dark alley, he stood in front of a shop.

"What are you willing to trade for your desire?"

Rayve's ability tore the Seed open again, and it dropped Ross, who scrambled backward, half-whimpering, half-laughing.

The Seed had eyes only for its Master, rearing its head forward, waving its half-blown arms.

"What's happening to me?" He gasped, crawling away from his Seed as fast as he could.

Only to find himself blocked by Rin. She stood in his way, expressionless.

"Get out of the way! It-It's trying to eat me!" he said, voice rising with desperation. He clutched his head. "I think there's something wrong with me. It must be the cause!"

He was losing his sanity, but not all of it, and the sane parts were collapsing as they attempted to digest what was happening. It would probably be a mercy for him to lose it all, but a Seed was not kind by nature. The more corrupted the Master's mind, the more anguish the Seed elicited, and the more benefits it reaped.

Rin was glad this Seed left its Master to drown in his well-deserved horror.

"What's wrong? Why are you afraid?" She tilted her head. "Isn't it your precious pet? The pet that ate up your wrongdoings, so that you could live your wealthy life well?"

"I'll be happy to assist in any way I can."

"We'll be counting on you, then."

He opened the door to the morgue. A blast of cold air greeted him.

She was crying her heart out over the old man.

"What a pity. I quite liked you. If only you hadn't stuck your nose where you didn't belong."

She turned around and glared at him.

"You killed him."

The words glanced off him like rainwater on windscreen.

Did he? He was not the one who did it. His hands were not covered with blood. It was the Seed.

The look on her face when she saw it was priceless.

"See, I told you I'm invincible."

Rin took a step forward, and he backed away.

"Do you not know the consequences of feeding a Seed? Someone as meticulous as you, how could you possibly miss it?"

Another step.

"Do you know what gourmet is in the Seed's eyes? Its Master. It saves the best for last."

Another step.

"Aren't you glad? This is its way of saying thank you for feeding it so well."

"Please, save me," Ross whispered. He lurched forward, trying to grab at Rin's ankle.

She stepped out of his reach. "Don't touch me with those filthy hands. How many people did you kill?"

He cocked his head, eyes wide. "It wasn't me. The monster – the monster is the one."

Of course, a man with such repulsive Pulses knew no remorse.

"They lied to me." His eyes were unfocused with terror.

They?

He giggled. "Do you know there's a shop that sells you everything you want as long as you pay?"

"And what did you pay them?"

He held both arms out. "Everything."

He probably sold his soul to the devil.

"Do you want to know where it is?" He giggled again and beckoned to her. "The –"

A deafening crash cut his words short, and a swirling cloud of dust billowed behind Ross. The Seed was on the ground, bearing a couple more canyons in its torso. Rayve was standing over it, livid.

The noise snapped Ross out of his frenzied reverie and with a whimper, he scrambled away from the Seed.

As though nothing happened, the Seed got to its feet and loomed over its Master.

Screaming and backed into a wall with nowhere left to run, Ross could only watch with bulging eyes as the claws reached for him once more.

"Save me!" His legs dangled helplessly in mid-air.

The Seed's jaw cracked wide open as it brought its Master closer, closer -

"No! Stop!" Looking down at Rin, he screamed, "Save me! I'll tell you! I'll tell you!"

Rin did not move a muscle. "I'm sorry, I'm not interested."

"You are! You will be!" He bawled, his voice an octave higher before breaking into a high-pitched scream.

He was inches away from its teeth when a massive force field rent the Seed in two.

Rayve stood across the Seed, panting with one hand on his side. Three overlapping Magic Circles glowed in front of him.

Ross slipped from its loosened claws and fell onto the rubble. Cracks formed over the Seed's exposed essence. It shuddered and broke.

The Seed's body disintegrated like ashes blown by the wind as debris and red shards rained down.

*

The building that was once a bistro was a sorry sight, its distinctive architecture ruined. Curious onlookers gathered around, tiptoeing for a better view and sharing speculations. The injured were tended to. The Council arrived shortly to escort the two Masters for questioning.

The three of them stood at a distance. Disheveled hair, smudged faces, with dusty and rumpled clothes, they looked like treasure hunters who had spent an entire year underground.

"I suppose it'll be a long time before he sees the sun again," Hayle said as the Council vehicle left the site. "And I hope she'll be able to move on too."

He sounded like the protagonist in the last episode of a television show who had to send a friend off to a new beginning.

Rin recalled how soulless Lyndia's eyes looked. She decided not to say anything.

Some scars would always bleed, no matter how much time had passed. She secretly wondered if she would be better off gaining closure by committing the crime regardless of the outcome of the action.

"Such a fearsome Seed in the hands of someone like him. I can't believe it was able to hide its existence up until recently, and that was only because the Council was investigating Miss Lyndia and her motives."

Henry Ross was too blind to realize that he was not the only one in possession of a Seed. Evil deeds bred grudges, and grudges sowed hatred, which in turn cultivated Seeds.

Rin drew in a deep breath and exhaled, worn out. "I'm leaving."

"Why are you the one tired when we were the ones doing all the fighting?" Rayve rounded on her. "Why did you not do anything when the Seed got him? Even with all those memory fragments – and I know we said earlier that we'll handle him – you were right there when the Seed got him! Were you really planning to let the Seed eat him?"

Rin glanced away, muttering, "For someone like him, it wouldn't be a bad idea."

Rayve's mouth opened and closed, but no words came.

She started to walk away, but not before the words that had been hanging at the tip of her tongue finally came out. "I don't know what you're after, but whatever you're doing right now, you'd better stop before it's too late."

It was directed at Rayve.

Rayve's expression grew several shades darker.

Hayle, on the other hand, was utterly clueless, looking back and forth between his twin and Rin's retreating form.

CHAPTER SIX

In the back of the Council vehicle heading towards headquarters, it was ghastly quiet. One of them was knocked out cold, the other one refused to speak a word to the escorts.

The escort guard looked back once in a while. The lights were turned off. He just had a heavy meal courtesy of his team leader and was feeling woozy.

He turned around, the seatbelt tight against his belly. "Hey, you all right there?"

There was no reply.

"Hey."

There was a sniff, followed by a hiccough.

The guard faced the front and shook his head.

Poor girl. So young to give up her life to an abomination. He had flipped through her file briefly and learned that she was an orphan who was raised by her grandfather and had her sole caretaker, her remaining family member murdered by a cold-blooded employer.

The drinks he had during dinner promoted a sense of philanthropy. He retrieved the sausage roll he bought in the afternoon and held it out to the back. "Look, I've got some food here. Do you want some?"

Another hiccough after a short pause, but no reply.

The guard waited for a moment and decided that it was a no. He leaned back in his seat and closed his eyes.

Another hiccough.

Then another.

And another.

He reopened his eyes, a frown forming between his brows. It was getting way too frequent.

Another hiccough.

Louder.

She sounded like she was choking.

The guard fumbled for the lights.

The man was sprawled on his side, still unmoving. The girl was hunched over, gasping and gagging. Black smog shrouded her body.

He hit the alarm switch, and a siren rang out. The high-pitched wail tore the silence of the night as the vehicle sped through the empty highway – a signal welcoming disaster.

The vehicle swerved wildly, tires screeching, and crashed into the divider, throwing the guard against the side door. His head hit the metal railing with a thump.

Another ear-splitting crash followed by a sharp, grating sound. The smell of smoke crept up his nostrils. Vision spinning and partially obscured by thick blood flowing down from his forehead, he was greeted by an unbelievable sight.

Something invisible was ripping the roof of the vehicle apart, exposing the inky sky beyond.

The first thought that crossed his mind was, *We're being hijacked.*

It was a ridiculous line of thought – this vehicle belonged to the highest authority of Ilias – yet the unbelievable was happening.

A small figure stood at the edge of the torn roof – a boy no older than eight.

He held out a hand.

The girl floated towards him, her fingers feebly clawing at her neck.

The moment they were at eye level, he plunged a hand into her chest as though it was fluid and drew out a black crystal.

Her head was thrown back, eyes staring at nothingness. A soundless cry escaped her lips. Her body grew limp like a puppet with its strings cut.

The guard fumbled for his communication device. He had to inform headquarters -

The child's head turned towards him, and for a terrible moment, the guard thought, *I'm going to die.*

The moment passed. Nothing happened.

The child flicked his wrist. Blackness obscured the guard's vision.

The charred smell grew stronger.

Then, he felt nothing at all.

The mysterious child let the girl fall.

She hit the floor like a wasted ragdoll, unmoving, hair splayed out in a fan beneath her.

CHAPTER SEVEN

The bell rang for lunch. Rin jerked awake as though hit in the head by an unpleasant alarm clock. The sounds of excited chatter filled her ears. She leaned back in her chair as her classmates filed past her out of the class.

Rin hardly ever fell asleep in class. She attributed the excessive drowsiness to the lack of sleep accumulated over the past week. As she began her solitary journey to the cafeteria, she heard someone call her name.

"Elziel!"

Rin sighed, increasing her pace. She had given him the slip in the morning, but he was clearly waiting to ambush her during lunch hour.

"Stop right there, Elziel!"

A scrawny boy wedged his way through a group of students hanging around in the corridor. His hair stood out in all directions, and he carried a hefty sling bag almost twice his width.

"You people owe me." He caught up with her, pushing his glasses that were falling off his nose. "Three times! I provided you with information three times! Nobody works for free!"

Ryan Joo tailed her as closely as he could all the way to the lunch queue, his large glasses slipping off his nose while giving her a lecture about the importance of timely payments and the possibility of charging interests for future transactions.

A second year from the IT division by day, his unassuming, studious facade successfully concealed the fact that he was an information broker by night. None of his classmates knew he ran a stall in the infamous black market during the weekends, trading currencies for pieces of information.

He had two principles. First: information was a priceless tool. Second: no bargaining.

Ryan was very confident in his abilities – and Rin had to admit, he was good at what he did. The problem was, he was a very persistent debt collector.

The lunch queue moved like an exhausted tortoise.

Unable to stand with Ryan hissing down her neck, she snapped around and growled, "Two out of three times, I am not the one asking for information. Ask the people who hired you."

Ryan made an irritated noise. "I barely see them more than twice a month. Aren't you three a team?"

"That doesn't mean the remaining member is liable," Rin said, equally annoyed. "Look, they'll be back soon. Just wait a little longer."

To Rin's absolute distaste, Ryan resolutely stuck to her as she made her way toward an empty table with her lunch. It wasn't that she disliked him. It was just that she simply disliked being forced to stay in the company of someone she shared almost nothing in common with.

Ryan retrieved his laptop from his bag and began working on his assignment over lunch while mumbling jargon that were foreign to her ears. Once in a while, he would direct a question at her, and she didn't understand half the things he said. She sat in her chair, picking at her cold chicken while contemplating how to get rid of this uninvited company when -

"Rin!"

A clear voice rose above the noise of the crowd, loud enough to turn heads.

There was a flash of strawberry blonde while everyone else made way. Rin ducked her head as eyes trained on her. A familiar scent of rosemary and a pair of arms flung themselves around her neck as thick, wavy pink hair tumbled over her shoulders. Maybelle nuzzled her with affection.

Rin debated if being dragged into unwanted attention by this flashy greeting was any better than enduring lunch with Ryan.

Maybelle Catherine Ilsa Lent was part-royalty, a second year in the administrative division, and Edwin's girlfriend. Glowing skin, blue eyes, and wavy hair that reached her slender waist, she was the center of attention wherever she went. Her mother was the king's cousin, and her father was the Duke of Creave. Her elegant self was reserved for formal occasions, prim and proper as the refined lady she was brought up as. Her true self loved feeding Rin and had zero mercy toward her boyfriend.

As confident as she was, there was one thing she was insecure about: her height, which was slightly over five feet.

"Hello, Mr. Joo," she said cheerily. "Rare to see you in Rin's company."

"Hello, Lady Lent," Ryan said stiffly.

Maybelle ignored the colorless greeting as she slid into the seat beside Rin and placed a lunch box in front of them. Rows of beautifully-made egg rolls and sandwiches filled the box. "I cannot decide which you like more. The eggs? The sandwiches? Both? Just take them all!" She beamed at Rin.

Rin ate a piece of Maybelle's egg rolls. Pleasantly soft with just the right tinge of salt and pepper, clearly putting their school's lunch to shame.

"You must've been busy. I overheard my mother saying that there's an exponential increase in the number of people affected by Seeds. The Council office is up to the neck with reports," Maybelle said, observing Rin fondly as she plucked a sandwich from the collection.

"It seems. They're putting up more jobs too." She took a bite of the sandwich – tuna and mayonnaise with a refreshing burst of cucumbers and tomatoes. Good.

"That also means I'll see less of the three of you." Maybelle sighed.

Every year, the Council held special exams to recruit high school students into their accelerated courses. These students were split into divisions depending on abilities and personal interests. The divisions included Hunting, IT, administration, research, and health studies. Upon completion of their studies, they would be assimilated into appropriate Council services.

Rin was a second-year student in the Hunting division, while Kazu and Edwin were in their third year. Being childhood friends, the trio were also teammates, working under the same mentor. Every completed assignment earned them points, and for the second year in a row, they were at the top of the leaderboard. Rin personally had no interest in ranks, but Edwin, with competitive fire in his veins, had no intention of giving up their spot to anyone else.

"Are you not eating?" Rin asked.

Maybelle shook her head, fiddling with the charms on Rin's bracelet. "I have. My morning classes ended earlier today."

She sat up straight and grabbed Rin's arm. "I just recalled something –"

Unease assaulted Rin. Whatever it was, if it had Maybelle's eyes glowing in excitement, it couldn't be good.

"Have you heard of a shop that grants your wishes for hearts?"

Ryan stopped tapping on his keyboard to stare at her.

"The requester pays an equivalent price in hearts. If he is unable to pay up, a guardian of the underworld will appear and drag him into the unknown, and no one hears of him again."

Maybelle had an undying interest in the supernatural and a knack for finding strange stories that defied laws of logic and magic from the net – which she kept a collection of. The problem was, more than half the stories were made up. The last time she led them on one of her excursions to uncover the truth, she made them hide in an alley the entire winter night to catch a "midnight bus to nowhere." Rin remembered dozing off on her feet and waking up at sunrise, the tips of her fingers blue and not a single vehicle in sight.

If Edwin had been there, he would've put his foot down, and they would both start fighting, while Kazu would try to be the peacemaker.

The problem was, they *weren't* there, and Rin had no idea how to react.

If such a shop did exist, Rin was ready to bet her entire week of lunch boxes that it was the doing of a Seed.

It was Ryan who spoke up.

"I've heard of it. Rumors have been circulating about a shop that grants wishes in return for hearts."

That was unexpected.

"Oh?" Maybelle sat up straight. "Do enlighten us, Mr. Joo."

"There are speculations of its possible locations. One of which is Osmanthus Street, which made it to the top ten of the Monthly Hottest Attractions of Ilias. A year ago, nobody had heard of it. The street was falling apart, barely able to sustain its business. All of a sudden, it gained traction and exploded in popularity."

Maybelle nodded in acknowledgment. "I see. What about the other locations?"

"There's also the -" Ryan clamped up, narrowing his eyes at Maybelle. His glasses slid off his nose again. "You're tricking me into spilling information, aren't you, Lady Lent? I was planning to sell it after getting enough to put things together. I would not impart my hard work free of charge!"

He stood up, insulted. Slamming his laptop shut, he gathered his belongings and left his half-eaten lunch in a huff.

"Wait, Mr. Joo," Maybelle held out a hand. "If you're talking about payment, I could always -"

"He's not talking about money," Rin said. "For people like him, they want something else."

"Oh, *that*," Maybelle said. "Well, it's all right. I'll glean the information myself."

Rin was amazed at how she perked up almost immediately. But what Maybelle said stirred up a piece of memory. She was strangely reminded of what Ross said in between the periods of lucidity and insanity.

"Do you know there's a shop that sells you everything you want as long as you pay?"

"And what did you pay them?"

"Everything."

If that was the shop that Maybelle meant, there was indeed a possibility that Ross traded his heart away.

A shadow loomed over Rin's plate, and she raised her head.

Rayve stood next to the table, looking like he had swallowed a mouthful of lemon gummies. Hayle lurked behind him, waving over his shoulder.

Being nice as she was, Maybelle responded in kind.

Rayve ignored both of them. "I just thought you might want to know. The Council vehicle carrying the two Masters last night met an accident – or that's what they were planning to tell the public."

Rin's fork slid from her fingers and hit her plate with a twang.

Maybelle glanced back and forth between Rayve and Rin, curious.

"From what we heard, the vehicle was hijacked. When reinforcements arrived at the scene, all they found was smoking wreckage."

"What about those two?"

Hayle shook his head. "We don't have conclusive information, but there was no news of survivors..."

"Who did it?" It was a rhetorical question – not one that Rin expected answers.

Rayve shrugged, turning to leave. "Beats us. This piece of news is classified, mind you. We aren't supposed to tell anyone about it, but Hayle insisted you would want to know."

The news robbed Rin of her appetite.

CHAPTER EIGHT

Rin did not expect taking Maybelle's story seriously. She wondered if it was curiosity or exhaustion that made her lose her mind – choosing crowded streets over sleep.

It bothered her.

The Master who couldn't see his flaws till the very end. The Master who was wronged, sought revenge the wrong way, and failed. The news of the hijacking and the fact that the rumored Heart Shop was in the very same town.

It seemed too much of a coincidence.

Or maybe, they were not coincidences to begin with.

Friday night along Osmanthus Street was packed full of people enjoying its vibrant energy and bustling activity. Couples going out for dates, friends heading towards arcades and cafes, business partners heading over to pubs for celebratory drinks. Shops and restaurants with discount banners, massage parlors with hourly rates, mascots holding welcome placards – all of them calling for customers. Red and yellow lanterns stretched overhead. Neon sign boards flashed from all directions. Music blasted in her ears. A flurry of drumbeats outside a shop and loud cheers added to the din.

A woman chattering excitedly into her phone, carrying more than ten shopping bags, squeezed between Rin and a lamppost to get into a boutique.

"Would you like some jerky? Freshly made today!" A cheery, red-faced man in a checkered apron shoved a plate of free samples in Rin's face.

"Come, come, join us at our grand opening! We have freebies for everyone!"

The street was like a friend with too much energy to burn. There was far too much movement, too much for her eyes to catch. When she looked ahead, all she saw were people zigzagging through the crowd in all directions. When she looked down, she saw pairs and pairs of feet hurrying about. It made her dizzy and cranky.

Someone grabbed her hand. Startled, Rin spun around.

It was a girl, about ten years old. Her brown bob was disheveled, stray strands plastered to her face. Her cheeks were flushed, and her shoulders heaved from running. The girl looked up. Prominent dark circles ringed her wide eyes.

Two things registered in Rin's mind. The first was how bizarre the sight of this girl was in this merry, colorful street with its joyful people.

The second was how empty her eyes were.

The girl's mouth moved.

"Help me."

What?

Someone bumped into Rin, nearly stepping on her foot as they walked past.

When she regained her balance, the girl was gone.

"Young missy." One of the salesmen approached her, carrying a tray of pickled samples. "Would you like to try some? We are running a flash sale-"

Rin ignored him, turning on the spot to look for the girl.

The usual crowded street. No one seemed to notice anything.

Had she imagined it?

*

Rin had no idea how she found it. She just did.

The sign, bordered by blinking tiny red neon lights, read, *The Heart Shop.*

It made no effort to hide itself. Located in a relatively quiet alley in the heart of Osmanthus Street, the shop was – like its brethren – unassuming and almost disappointingly normal, unlike the ones competing to stand out in the main street. A set of tinted glass doors concealed the interior. Another smaller sign beneath the blinking one read *OPEN.*

There was not a hint of Seed in the vicinity. Only the smell of charred meat from the kitchen of the nearby restaurant lingered. The music from the main street sounded far away.

She halted at the doors, rather uncertain. Should she go in?

Rin hardly ever hesitated, but this entire affair felt rather odd and, she quite hated to admit, stupid.

The sign winked at her, inviting her in.

Pushing her thoughts aside, she slid the doors open.

CHAPTER NINE

It was a cold, overcast night. The dense, turbulent clouds painted the sky an uneasy grey, concealing the moon. The autumn wind blew, bringing with it the scent of impending rain. An empty can rattled over the pavement.

Within the walls of a certain apartment at the end of Osmanthus Street, its inhabitants were in deep slumber.

The wind kicked up, howling as it rushed beneath crevices.

Somewhere, a door slammed. Shadows came to life. First, a flicker of movement. Then, they grew – longer, bigger – and peeled themselves off the surfaces.

An old tree branch snapped and fell off with a thud.

In one of the rooms up above, a young lady woke. Still wrapped in the warmth of a blissful dream, she turned over and snuggled close to her fiancé, the sheets settling atop her bare skin. She was about to drift away when she picked up an unusual odor.

Overwhelmingly metallic.

Then, she heard a sound. Something squelched. Her eyes flew open and she propped herself up -

And saw blood.

So much blood.

Splattered carelessly over the wallpaper, the floor, across the ceiling.
Her fiancé lay unmoving, his eyes all white. A thick, dark liquid frothed out of his gaping mouth.

His chest was torn open, a huge cavity with nothing discernible within. What looked like bits and pieces of his innards spilled over the sheets. Something invisible was moving, picking at his entrails. Making those wet sounds. Horror rose like bile in her throat, squeezing her windpipe.

A clank. A twitch in the shadow. She turned.

Her eyes flared wide at what she saw– threadlike fingers at the rim of an agape mouth. *Something was trying to made its way out.*

Kicking the sheets aside, she screamed as it plunged towards her.

She screamed and screamed.

No one heard her.

CHAPTER TEN

The tinkling of wind chimes blended into the peaceful summer afternoon as the warm breeze caressed her hair. Crickets orchestrated a choir in the hedges. The trees in her grandmother's backyard rustled, showing off luscious green leaves.

She sat on the side porch, making shapes with bands that would not obey her fingers.

"Rei, Rei," she called, holding up a misshapen tangle. "Where do I go from here?"

Her older brother crouched next to her, putting down the book he was reading and smiling. "You missed a step. Here, let's begin from scratch."

He picked up two bands from the ground and showed her the steps, waiting patiently as she retraced his moves. The star she had been trying to make finally took shape.

"I did it!" She beamed.

He laughed at her excitement. "Let me show you something." He placed their bands together and guided her fingers over the loops and twists. "Now look, what is it?"

She cocked her head. "A flower?"

He laughed again. "No, silly." He stretched his end. The bands pulled out into an intricate, layered pattern. "A spider web."

"Oh! That's pretty!"

Rei took the bands from her hands. One of her fingers slipped, and the bands straightened out, the pattern ruined.

Aw, they would have to redo it -

Her brother was gone.

"Rei?"

She was no longer in the backyard. The wind became a gale, whipping around her, and the rustling grew louder and louder, filling her ears.

Oh, no.

The trail of bright red blood in front of her invited her somewhere.

Not again.

Her body moved despite her protests, following the trail.

No.

She could see from the corners of her eyes. The scene she revisited over and over again.

Wake up.

In the middle of a Magic Circle, there was a limp figure. The figure looked up. It was her brother's face – pale, drained, hollow.

She scrunched her eyes tight.

The image of his face burned into the back of her eyelids –

Wake up!

– which distorted and morphed again into a pallid mask floating in the darkness –

*

The alarm clock went off. The noise shrilled throughout her room, breaking the silence of the serene morning and hurting her ears.

A hand fumbled for it and managed to find the correct button.

Rin blinked dazedly at the sunlight streaming through her windows. Then she caught sight of the time. Half past nine.

She sat up, only to find her sheets holding her in a determined tangle. Her game console slid off the bed and landed on the floor. She had fallen asleep at four after matching thousands of tiles, and now her head spun.

When she went down to the kitchen to grab some breakfast, the television was on.

"This makes the fifth person reported missing within the last two weeks. Local authorities are growing increasingly concerned over the incident, raising the possibility of the involvement of Seeds. Council Hunters on site refused to comment on the incidents, citing that nothing conclusive has been obtained -"

The broadcaster's voice was interrupted by the occasional thuds Mirelle made. She was ironing wrinkles out of a shirt as though it owed her a hundred years' worth of wages. This was probably one of the rare occasions she was fighting with Cnaris.

"He thinks he knows everything about cleaning, does he?" she muttered under her breath, her arms moving in and out sharply. "The ungrateful clean freak. I will empty those shelves of books. Books he keeps for collecting – collecting dust. Now, what is wrong with the iron today?"

Rin inched behind her. "You forgot to switch it on."

Mirelle looked at the iron, at the switch, and then at the shirt. She drew a deep breath and set the iron down on the board so hard that it nearly fell over. Rin jumped.

The doorbell rang – very loudly, very rudely, and with very bad timing.

A pause, and then it rang again.

Mirelle's expression grew darker. Whoever it was, the unfortunate soul was going to face her wrath if she opened the door. People who hardly got angry were the scariest when they did.

"I'll get it," Rin said quickly.

The bell rang again. The noise reverberated through the walls. There were only two types of people who would resort to ringing the doorbell in such a manner: an impatient client with a self-proclaimed emergency, or a foolish delivery man with a death wish.

"*Who in the hell is trying to break my doorbell?*" Cnaris roared from his study.

Rin opened the door. The bell stopped.

There was no one outside.

No client, no delivery man.

Instead, a simple envelope lay on the doorstep. The edges were rimmed with gray lines.

It was addressed to her:

Rin Elziel
Shortbread Factory
Behind Hillstone Lane
Creave

Rin picked it up and opened it. Inside was a piece of paper that bore a message in elaborate, cursive font:

This receipt is hereby a confirmation of your transaction of xxx heart in return for xxxx. Our collectors will be retrieving the set amount of heart in due time. Thank you for your patronage.

Sincerely,
The Heart Shop

P.S. Transaction details are blanked out to safeguard the client's confidentiality in rare occasions where the receipt falls into hands other than the client's.

She stared at it for a whole minute, reading the words over and over again.

How did the shop know her real name and address when she disclosed neither?

CHAPTER ELEVEN

Rayve did not believe in weather forecasts.

Once, it promised a sunny weekend, ideal for flower gazing and picnics. A younger Hayle and Rayve had been looking forward to it. Their mentor planned an outing for them as a treat after an entire week of training. When the time came, thunder crashed and lightning flashed. The torrential rain washed all the flowers away, and Hayle was miserable for the rest of the following week. Another time, it predicted hail, and Rayve had to put off his Hunting plans and stayed indoors for the rest of the day at Hayle's insistence, and he waited and waited for the hail that never came.

Today, it predicted rain in the evening. It was a clear fall day with not a hint of rainclouds. Hayle was down with a cold, sneezing since he woke up and using up the entire box of tissues within half a day. Rayve was on the way back from the pharmacy to buy some medicine when it began to pour, soaking him from head to toe in seconds.

Curses. He ran the last half mile back to their temporary rental house, stopping under the balcony to shake water droplets off his hair and clothes before heading in.

Hayle gave him a dismayed greeting, lamenting that Rayve was next in the line to get a cold, and insisted that he take a shower before doing anything else.

By the time Rayve got out of the shower, Hayle had taken his medicine and tucked himself into bed.

Rayve sighed. Hayle was always trying not to make him worry. Yet, he made Rayve worry all the time.

Their master was away for the entire month. He had the tendency to vanish now and then, leaving them instructions for their next assignments via text or phone calls. He also liked moving on a whim. Now, he was renting them a townhouse in the middle of an unassuming town with easy access to whatever facilities they needed, promising them a proper home by spring.

Rayve didn't mind not having a proper place to stay. After all, he was used to living in poverty for a long time. As long as Hayle was fine, he was too.

Their bedroom was on the first floor, a simple, plain space with wood finishing and barely any furnishing. Just two beds, a closet, and a window overlooking the street. The orange streetlamp directly outside peered in, benevolently offering its illumination over the floorboards.

He went to check on Hayle, reaching out to touch his forehead. Luckily, no temperature.

"You don't have to worry so much, you know. I'm not a kid anymore." Hayle's head-cold voice came from beneath the blankets.

Rayve did not expect him to be awake. "I know."

Hayle turned over so that he was looking at Rayve. "You should start taking better care of yourself too."

"I know."

He knew Hayle knew he did not really mean what he said. To be honest, Rayve had no idea what he meant either.

Hayle's eyes were earnest. "I want to be of use to you and the master, not a burden."

Rayve knew Hayle did not like being dependable, and he knew sooner or later, he could no longer stop Hayle from doing what he wanted to do.

But there was just one thing. Something he had to do for Hayle. And he thought Hayle would want it too.

"Are you listening? Rayve?"

Rayve gave a start. Hayle was waving his hand in front of his face.

"What's wrong? You were staring into space. Is something bothering you?"

Tactful Hayle always realized if Rayve was troubled; he would feel the same, and it would be reflected on his face.

"It's nothing," Rayve shifted. "I'm just thinking about the calculus question this afternoon."

Hayle wasn't gullible; he was just easily distracted.

"Oh, no," Hayle groaned, rubbing his eyes with his knuckles. "Did the teacher cover a difficult topic today? Man, I suck at math. Now I'll have to catch up."

Rayve was lying. Hayle was right – he was bothered. He glanced out of the window – the rain had subsided into a drizzle. The streetlamp winked at him through the glass, drenched in solitude.

"Have you..." Rayve began. "Have you, by chance, felt strange or different recently?"

"If you mean the cold, yes. My eyes and nose can't stop itching, and my throat is sore-"

"No, I don't mean that. I mean-" He stopped himself. "Never mind."

"What is it?"

"Nothing, idiot," Rayve said with an edge of affection. "Just go to sleep."

The medicine must have made him drowsy because Hayle obliged.

Rayve sat by the edge of the bed for a long time after his brother dozed off.

Whatever you're doing right now, you'd better stop before it's too late.

Rin Elziel's words echoed in his ears. It shouldn't have bothered him that much, yet it did. After all, what did she know?

It was just... Sometimes, he found Hayle looking rather out of sorts when he was alone –staring at the wall, wandering around aimlessly –

Rayve stood up, switched off the lights, and climbed into his own bed.

It was just a coincidence, right?

Somehow, he couldn't fully convince himself that he was overthinking, and the question bugged him all the way to sleep.

When he woke up to the cold dawn the next morning, the first thing he saw was an empty bed with the blankets thrown off.

Hayle was gone.

CHAPTER TWELVE

Rin spent the next few days bugged by a string of strange, petty incidents. The receipt made a habit of showing itself everywhere she went – between the pages of her book, underneath her breakfast plate, stuck on the window, on the mirror of the washroom -

She always ripped it off in annoyance.

She even burned it. Rin generally disliked using her ability wantonly. The Sacred Fire had the ability to devour anything and everything and naturally attracted Seeds and occasionally greedy hearts who coveted the ability. The receipt, however, seemed to possess an ability to replicate itself beforehand, so by the time she ignited the fourteenth copy into oblivion and attracted a swarm of wasp-like Seeds, she gave up.

Rin had no idea how it was going to collect the debt from her. Neither had she any idea what it felt like to lose a portion of her heart. She was starting to feel that the entire affair was a mistake, a self-dug pit of trouble.

To add to her ire, there was a very, very faint presence of Seed that forever lingered about her.

It was like an additional sense she developed over the years of Hunting. Each Seed had a unique aura, like humans and thumbprints. She couldn't help but feel this one was rather familiar.

Cnaris, of course, was incensed.

"Whatever it is, I want it out of my house by this weekend," he snapped.

Between the schoolwork she missed and library duties, she barely had time to return to Pallin.

The last straw was, however, on Thursday afternoon.

She was heading towards the bakery to collect the bread Mirelle ordered the day before. A loose newspaper tossed around by the wind wrapped itself around her boots. She bent down to remove it. The headline read, *Man Found in Gruesome -*

Movement ahead caught her eye.

Just five feet in front of her, at the junction where the florist was, she saw him.

Her heart missed a beat.

His lean figure, his high school uniform, and the red hair the precise shade as hers were just like how she remembered. He was talking on the phone and laughing, walking past the junction into the next street – away from her.

Wait -

Rei! The name nearly left her lips when she regained her senses and stopped herself. She lowered her hand, fingers curling against her palm.

The last time she saw him had been five years ago. For five years, she kept his memory deep in the recesses of her heart. What was left were fragments of what she remembered of him. She would someday forget him, and the prospect of it scared her.

And there he was earlier, as though he had walked right out of her memories to remind her -

It's impossible. It's not him.

Rei was dead.

Her momentary shock turned into anger.

"Would you let me look into your heart?"

It invoked a raw emotion inside her that she had almost forgotten. How dare it use the memory of her brother against her?

She stood rooted on the spot, seething. A single line of thought crossed her mind: *Whoever the mastermind is, they will pay a hefty price.*

*

Cnaris was in a foul mood from the Seed contamination, resorting to door slamming and fault-picking with every little thing – to Mirelle's chagrin, so she decided to head out to do some shopping. Rin's head pounded from the lack of sleep throughout the past week. Unable to stand the noise, she retired to her room.

Tumbling into bed felt like the best choice she had ever made. She closed her eyes, and sleep engulfed her almost immediately.

When she opened her eyes, she was standing on Osmanthus Street. The lights blinked overhead, and lanterns were suspended in midair, bright against the night sky. Promotions and discounts blared on loudspeakers. Troupes of dancers performing in front of a shop celebrated its grand opening, their lavish dresses swishing to the beat.

A hand grabbed hers. She looked down.

It was the same girl – with hollow eyes and an expressionless face.

"Help me," the girl said.

The owner of the jerky shop came up to her, beaming, and held up a tray with a single platter of samples in the middle. "Have a try, miss. Our products are freshly made."

The girl was gone.

The vibrant lights went off.

The people went lifeless – as though they ran out of battery. They stopped in their tracks, slumped against the walls, all with their heads hung low.

Silence fell like a dense, heavy blanket.

"Greetings, esteemed client."

Rin turned around.

Standing in the middle of the street where all life had halted was a sole figure wearing a bowler hat that covered his face.

She recognized his voice. The Manager of the Heart Shop.

He looked up.

Her heart dropped.

That pale visage akin to a mask, too smooth to be real. Eyes with hollow sockets. A crescent that represented his smiling mouth.

"Would you like to trade your heart?"

There was a crack, and every head in the vicinity whipped up in unison, staring in her direction – all wearing similar faces.

Before she could react, the Manager was in her face. "Would you like to trade your heart?"

This time, the voice was inside her ears.

She winced.

An invisible force coiled around her neck, and she reached for it, fingers wrapping around empty air.

Her feet slowly lifted off the ground –

*

Rin woke with a start.

She was still lying on her bed. Taking a few moments to calm herself, she pushed herself up.

Her headache worsened thanks to the nightmare, throbbing deep in her temples.

She headed to the washroom, deciding that a splash of water in the face would do some good. As she turned the tap on, she glanced at her reflection in the mirror.

At the sides of her neck, were bruises in the shape of fingers.

The doorbell rang, with urgency and desperation, but not the rude blaring as a few days back.

Mirelle was still out running grocery shopping. Cnaris was locked in his study, obviously not going to open the door, so Rin did, water dripping off the edge of her chin.

Rayve stood on the other side, hair tousled and clothes haphazardly thrown on. Worry painted his face, hiding a stronger emotion beneath his wide eyes and tense shoulders – fear.

"Please," he said between breaths. Rin wondered if he had run all the way. "I'd hate to ask but -"

He looked like he was struggling internally. Rin somehow guessed what he was going to say before the words left him.

"Please help Hayle."

CHAPTER THIRTEEN

Rayve led her, predictably, to Osmanthus Street.

He only said, "You'll understand," and refused to say another word after that. Rin allowed herself to follow. The puzzle pieces were somehow falling into place one after another without her having to do anything. It crossed her mind that it might be a trap, but she decided it was the most convenient course of action.

She planned to go after it anyway.

The day version of Osmanthus Street was dead and soulless. The lanterns that were part of the night revelry hung limp and faded overhead. The street itself was a picture of desolation, its shutters drawn and not a single soul in sight. A slight current stirred up dust from the ground. A lone empty paper bag skittered midway across the street and stopped.

The arch at the entrance to the street looked like an invitation to a ghost town. The barren tree next to it was almost sorry, spreading its empty arms in vain, longing for warmer weather where the greens would bud again.

She turned to Rayve. "I suppose you'll have to explain yourself now."

Except that he was no longer there.

Rin stared at the spot he had been standing for a couple of moments, trying to register something apart from a desire to utter an impolite word.

For one moment, she thought Rayve had ditched her – or pranked her.

The next moment, her rationale returned. What did she expect? She was heading into an area controlled by a Seed.

From the moment she stepped onto the street, she had already been inside the Seed's Territory.

Rin had taken part in too many assignments to count, slain countless Seeds throughout the five years she had been a Hunter. A Seed that could control almost half the town was not a trifling that sprouted out from the darkness of a single Master.

Because Seeds originated from humans, they had minds and wills of their own. Heading into a Territory of such scale alone was not exactly a brilliant idea.

Rin wasn't reckless; she just believed that opportunities were fleeting. They disappeared as fast as they presented themselves.

She wondered if Kazu and Edwin had seen the text message she sent them earlier. She also wondered if they would get angry.

Standing in the street, she felt exposed and strangely alone Her next logical course of action would be either to look for Rayve or the Heart Shop, neither of which seemed like something the Seed would let her accomplish easily.

The street layout was similar to what she remembered from her visit that night. The jerky shop, the grocery store, the video game store...

A whimper stopped her in her tracks. It came from the alley nearby.

Behind a pile of trash bags and discarded boxes stained with used oil and old juice, a dark red liquid spread over the ground, beneath the bags, seeping into crevices between the tiles.

Another whimper.

A sharp vision lanced through her – too fast and too brief to make out anything.

Her forehead broke out in cold sweat. She inadvertently took a step forward.

"It's no use," came a voice, startling her.

A girl emerged from behind a pillar two shops away. She had shoulder-length black hair with familiar, empty eyes surrounded by heavy eyebags. A filthy white frock torn at the edges hanging over her skinny shoulders. She wore a pair of flip-flops that were rather too big for her feet.

Rin's breath caught in her throat. "It's you."

"It's beyond saving. No need to ponder something that will soon disappear."

Her tone was light and matter-of-fact, like she was talking about the weather. It was unexpected, coming from a ten-year-old's mouth.

A heavy silence lingered between them.

"Are you a Hunter?" The girl asked.

Rin was not a trusting person. A girl emerging in the middle of a Territory was miles away from being trustable. She gathered her composure and opted to reply with another question.

"Why were you asking for help?"

The girl looked down at her feet, scuffing her flip-flops against the ground. "Bad things happen."

"What kind of bad things?"

"I... Something is stealing my heart."

"What is?"

"I don't know." She shrugged. Words poured out of her in a torrent. "It's...something. Everyone is becoming weird – my daddy, my big sister, and the uncle next door. They had their hearts stolen. I'm also becoming weird. I can feel it." She lifted her head. "I don't want to become like them."

It still bothered Rin how devoid of life the girl's eyes were. They were supposed to be alit with innocence and sparkle, looking forward to discovering the world. Instead, they were stagnant pools, dull and lifeless, as though her facial muscles had never learned how to tug at her eyebrows, her eyes, and her lips to form expressions.

A dissociation between words and expressed emotions was usually a sign of Seed influence.

But this girl carried no scent of Seed on her.

Rin decided it would be wiser to tread carefully. "And what happens if you lose it?"

The girl slowly withdrew several pieces of paper from the pocket of her frock and handed them to Rin.

Newspaper cuttings and handwritten notes.

"Please destroy that thing, big sister," she whispered, her gaze piercing into Rin.

"What are these–"

Then, somewhere, the clock struck seven.

And like a flipped switch, the entire town flared to life.

All the lights came on. The music started up. The shops were open for business as though they always had been. The street was packed with laughing and chattering visitors and hollering shop owners.

Lights floated in front of Rin's eyes, making her dizzy. Her mind struggled to process the sudden change.

"Come, big sister!" the little girl said, smiling and dancing around Rin, a completely different person. She held out her hands as though she was in an amusement park. "Let's play!"

A Territory was almost always bizarre, like an unusual dream with skipped sequences, random places, and unknown people who felt familiar. A Seed was not bound by rules; their existence was an abomination.

Within the space of their creation, they were the master, the rule-maker, the king.

Before Rin could answer, a lanky man she recognized as the owner of the gigantic toy shop at the junction approached them. He had high cheekbones and was all smiles, right up to his crow's feet.

"Hello, would you like to come by my place to play? I have a gift for you."

To Rin's surprise, the girl's cheeriness faded. She shot him a terrified look, backed away from the man, and fled into the crowd without glancing back.

CHAPTER FOURTEEN

Classes were over by the time Kazu and Edwin reported the completion of their assignment to the office.

"Lunch!" Edwin exclaimed. "I'm dying. I'm starved. I need food. It's the assignment's fault if I have to rely on antacids for the rest of my life."

The corners of Kazu's lips twitched. Edwin was exaggerating, just because he was expecting homemade food from a certain someone.

"We haven't eaten a proper meal since last week," Edwin half-groaned, clutching his stomach.

"Are you rehearsing a story to win over Maybelle's sympathy right now?"

Edwin cleared his throat and righted himself. "So that your recount will not contradict mine."

And he was shameless to boot.

"You've eaten four times, with an addition of three in-between-meal snacks every day while we were tracking the Seed-"

"Hush. When you get a girlfriend, you'll know how to play your cards properly."

Kazu was certain he was better off without that piece of advice.

Turning right at the junction leading to the cafeteria, they ran into a familiar face, whose expression turned sour at the sight of them. Kazu nudged Edwin in the ribs.

"Crap," Edwin muttered. Out aloud, he said, "Hiya, Ryan." He gave the underclassman a smack on the back. Ryan's thin frame lurched forward from the impact. "Why so gloomy?"

"Because yours truly is broke and is in great need of due payment." Ryan held out his hand. "Please."

Edwin clasped Ryan's fingers. "I'm so sorry to hear that. I'm sure they'll pay up soon."

Ryan bestowed him his best scowl.

Just then, Edwin spotted Maybelle waving from inside the cafeteria.

Sidestepping Ryan like he was a puddle of spilled juice on the floor, Edwin glided over to her, arms stretched out. "Hey, did you miss me?"

Maybelle glanced behind his shoulder. "Hello, Kazu. Glad to see you back. Is Rin with you?"

"Aren't you looking for the wrong person?" Edwin asked with a hint of reproach.

"Hi, Maybelle," Kazu replied, taking care to avoid Ryan's mutinous gaze as the latter stormed away.

Maybelle purposely ignored Edwin's statement. She slid into the seat she had reserved. A lunch box sat in front of her, filled with her signature egg rolls and sandwiches. "Too bad, I was planning to give them to Rin."

"Isn't this supposed to be *our* homecoming gift?" Edwin asked, incredulous.

"Well..." Maybelle considered. "It *is* your gift, but made in consideration of Rin's favorites."

Edwin was affronted.

Kazu burst out laughing. "Stop making fun of him. He was talking about you all week."

"Kaz-" Edwin warned between his teeth. The tips of his ears turned light pink.

Maybelle worked hard to hide a smile. Afterward, she pushed the lunch box an inch closer to Edwin. Their pull-and-push antics never failed to amuse.

Kazu excused himself to the counter to get himself some lunch, despite Maybelle's insistence that she made enough for all of them, and to give them both some alone time.

The cafeteria buzzed, chatter mingling into indiscernible sounds. In the distance, the PA system announced an upcoming club meeting that was half-lost to the din. The roasted chicken had been marinated with strong-smelling herbs and heaped with loads of garlic – something Rin would have hated, he considered. He deliberately took his time getting a drink and took a detour all around the packed cafeteria back to the table.

A normal day in school.

Some people minded mundane days, but Kazu liked them. He found such peaceful and laid-back days difficult to come by. Unlike Edwin, who was programmed with plenty of energy to expend and had an abundance of excitement to burn, Kazu preferred having quiet time spent with friends, family, and music.

When he arrived at the table, Edwin was telling an equally engrossed Maybelle about their previous assignment – undoubtedly with added flair and details that did not exactly happen.

"- the Seed sliced into two and words exploded out of it, alphabets and all, like fresh popcorn -"

Of course, time spent with Edwin was never exactly quiet.

"- and we were all blasted out of the Territory! Even the walls were broken -"

"You make it sound like we just faced a bomb." Kazu slid into the seat opposite him.

Edwin shook his head and said drily, "You need to learn the ways of storytelling."

He proceeded with his tale while Kazu worked on his lunch.

Once he was done, Maybelle glanced back and forth between them. "Hasn't it been becoming worse lately? Seeds seem to be appearing everywhere. It's like someone is trying to disseminate Seeds deliberately-" She broke off, biting her lip, throwing a guilty glance at Edwin.

Kazu carefully observed the pattern on his plate. Any topic related to Edwin's arrested father was taboo. For a moment, an awkward silence hung amidst them. Their neighboring table packed their bags and left with their trays, talking about upcoming tests.

Edwin faked a cough, breaking the tension. "I'm sure there are many people who would do anything for profit. The Master we spent the whole week tracking stole words and sold the words back to the people he stole them from."

The atmosphere returned to normal. Maybelle's relief was written all over her face.

Edwin plowed on. "Everyone used to accept that Seeds arise from negativity within human hearts until one day they found out that some were raised artificially from Sygns. Then, suddenly, people started questioning the origin of Seeds."

 "Why?"

"Because Seeds are not supposed to be manmade," Kazu answered, cutting his chicken into chunks and eating one. It was dry and over-seasoned. "But Sygns are."

A Sygn was the disguise of weapons, a miniature version of tools, or the concrete form of abilities. It usually took the form of a trinket or an everyday item. Kazu's Sygn was a necklace, holding the true form of his gun. Every Sygn was powered by a magic stone that granted it the aptitude to resonate with ability-users and the capacity to transform on command.

Edwin waved his hand. "That's what we were told. All the books are written as if magic is a definite set of laws and formulas. Boring. What a lack of creativity. Look, magic has infinite forms, uncontainable and overflowing with endless possibilities."

His tone emphasized his detest of textbooks.

"That's why I said 'supposed.'" Kazu said nonchalantly.

Edwin pointed the fork at him in approval, bits of egg dangling from the tip. "This is why we get along, buddy."

"It's hard to believe someone can actually create Seeds." Maybelle rested her chin on her hands. "They must be formidable."

"Considering how ridiculous some feats may sound, it's not impossible for someone to create Seeds and transform them into Sygns. Magic Circles originated from illegal practices of transmutation using human slaves as mediums, and there was a musician with the ability to converse with animals. He managed to conduct an orchestra consisting of cats and dogs, and made a fortune out of it."

Maybelle gaped. "I would like to know the musician's name-"

Edwin cut in before she could pursue the matter further, speaking between mouthfuls of eggs. "The point is, magic is like technology: you're just waiting for people to work their innovations, and boom, a new invention in the air."

"Can you swallow properly before you speak?"

Edwin obliged, gulping down the rest of his food. "Hence, my responsibility lies in uncovering the endless potentials of magic. I just came up with a new trick last night." He nudged Maybelle. "Wanna see?"

Maybelle stared at him almost pityingly. "If only you showed half as much effort in your homework."

"Homework is for the mundane. Also, homework is meant to be copied."

"That applies only to you."

"Assignments, on the other hand, are the opposite. They are proof of competency." Edwin's eyes gleamed. "We have plenty of rivalries, you know. I checked the board this morning. Thanks to Rin's toiling when we were gone, we're still on top. Number two is three thousand, four hundred fifty-two points away," he said as he glanced around.

Kazu knew he was looking to gloat at the Signon twins, but they were nowhere in sight.

"What do you get for being at the top of the list?" Maybelle asked.

Kazu shook his head. "Nothing, unless you count the prestige of being top of the year and the satisfaction that comes with it like Ed does."

Maybelle scrutinized him. "Why do I feel like there's something else in it for you?"

She was partly right. He smiled a knowing smile. "I just like the overall process of it."

Maybelle sighed. "You do love talking in riddles. But mystery also makes one more attractive. Here, have some of the sandwiches before Ed finishes them all."

She heaped the remaining sandwiches onto Kazu's plate before Edwin could touch them.

"I was going to take one!" Ed said indignantly.

Kazu secretly wondered if he was supposed to finish everything on his plate out of manners. "Shouldn't we leave some for Rin?"

Edwin glanced around. "Speaking of which, where did the stupid cat go? Lunch hour is almost over."

While they were talking, half the cafeteria had cleared.

Maybelle frowned. "I haven't seen her much this week. She's seemed bothered lately -" Her voice trailed away, muttering more to herself. "Right after I told her about the Heart Shop. She couldn't possibly have -"

Kazu developed an ominous feeling that he felt had very little to do with his lunch.

Edwin nearly dropped the last of his egg. "The heart what?"

"The Heart Shop. A shop that trades hearts for anything you wish for." She gave them furtive glances, expecting an outburst.

Edwin groaned. "Did you read those bogus stories again? Please don't tell me you're planning to trade your heart. Are you saying the stupid cat believed you and went searching for the shop?"

"How sure are you that it's a bogus story?" Maybelle challenged. She straightened her petite stature as much as she could.

"I haven't forgotten the midnight bus and the umbrella that changes weather every time you open it, princess," Edwin retorted. "Tell me, what is the point of trading hearts? How does anyone live without a heart in the first place?"

"You were the one talking about endless possibilities earlier."

"I was talking about legit magic – purposeful *and* justified. What do you think, Kaz?"

Kazu busied himself with the sandwiches and carefully declined to answer.

"Also, it is technically impossible to fulfill *any* wish because wishes are infinite and immeasurable." Edwin went on like an avid lecturer insisting his point. "Magic does not just create something out of nothing. The magic that grants wishes like a fairy godmother does not exist. If there were, I'll bet my whole year's wages that it's a Seed's doing."

Edwin reached for another egg roll.

Maybelle slapped his hand away. "They are not for you."

"Excuse me?"

"Not. For. You."

Edwin muttered something under his breath that sounded like, "Preposterous."

"Did you say something?" Maybelle gave him a smile that reduced him to silence.

Sometimes, Kazu wondered if Edwin and Maybelle found enjoyment in arguing with each other. Perhaps it was an expression of affection.

"Well, you might both be right," he said in a quiet, meditative voice, ready to pull back the moment they decided to pounce on him. "It might exist, and it might also be a Seed's doing."

"If it is a Seed's doing, then what is the stupid cat doing by going to an unreleased assignment all alone?" Edwin scowled.

Just then, Kazu's phone saved him. It vibrated, signaling an incoming text.

So did Edwin's.

He and Maybelle were busy glowering at each other, so Kazu checked his.

His fork slipped from his fingers, clattered over the edge of the table, and bounced off onto the ground.

The noise caught both Edwin and Maybelle's attention, their argument instantly forgotten.

"I think I have an idea where Rin is," Kazu said, looking up slowly. "And you two might just have hit the jackpot."

CHAPTER FIFTEEN

Mr. Nim's Toy Emporium was probably the biggest Rin had ever seen. A model railway track ran the entire length of the shop, equipped with shiny engines chuffing out tiny puffs of artificial smoke. Stations built out of Lego had miniature passengers alighting with luggage, uniformed porters, and whistle-blowing guards. A jigsaw puzzle depicting a fairy tale town was on display alongside a variety of board games that were mid-round. Picture cards decorated the side wall.

The only customers were children. Two were playing house at the play area. A younger boy ran around the store wearing a makeshift cloak and waving a plastic sword.

In the middle of the toy shop, a group of colorfully-dressed children wearing pointed hats danced around a fairy ring of plushies, trailing behind an equally colorful Mr. Nim, who was playing a merry melody on a flute. Rin supposed they were taking after elves or dwarves.

"Come join us, big sis!" one of them called out.

Rin did not answer. She was busy staring at the walls. They faded in and out. The train chuffed in exhaustion. One of the teddies keeled over, a beady eye loose. The picture of the jigsaw transformed into a sinister jungle with dim lamps lighting up a tiny path to nowhere. The brilliance of the emporium gave away momentarily, revealing its used, dilapidated interior.

None of the children seemed to realize anything.

She supposed they were bewitched into thinking it was a toy paradise. She was exempted because she was an uninvited guest.

A girl with a pair of ponytails came up to her, holding a set of cards. She looked about six. "Let's play, big sis."

She had a strange smile. Crooked, hesitant, and forced. Her wide eyes gazed tremulously at Rin.

It took Rin a short while to realize that it was fear.

Leaning down, she said in a low voice, "Do you not want to be here?"

The girl gave an imperceptible shake of her head, looking more frightened than ever.

"Why can't you leave?"

She glanced to the left. Rin followed her gaze.

The picture cards earlier were actually photographs – each one of a child. All of them had the same fake smile plastered on their faces.

"I want to go home, Mister," the boy with the cloak wailed, running up to Mr. Nim.

The toy shop owner bent down to speak to him, his face inches away. "Oh, no, dear. You have not had enough fun yet."

"No! I wanna go home!" The boy threw the cloak down in temper and ran towards the exit.

Right before he reached it, he disappeared. The cloak and sword clattered to the floor.

At the same time, a new photograph appeared on the wall.

It was of the boy struggling to free himself from the constraints of the frame. His movements slowed until he finally stopped moving, lips curved upwards in a forced smile.

The girl turned away in fright.

Mr. Nim's voice echo softly around the shop:

Oh, dear child, I just want your smile.

Rin glanced down at her hand. She was still holding on to the papers she had been given earlier.

The topmost one read, *Missing Children.* Below it was a list of names. Dates were written next to each one, all within the same month.

"Hello, hello." Mr. Nim came up to her. "Are you enjoying yourself?"

Rin did not bother looking up. In a low voice, she said, "Mister, did you trade your heart?"

There was a broad smile in his voice. "Yes, I wished to preserve the smiles of children."

Because I couldn't keep my child's.

"These little ones are so precious." He clasped his hands over his chest.

Precious? Keeping them as prisoners?

"Daddy, I want that robot! Timmy's dad got him the whole set for his birthday. Why can't I have one?"

Business was not good. Money was short. "It is expensive, dear. Maybe next time."

"No! You always say the same thing! You're lying!"

Then, just weeks later, a child running after a ball in the street, a screech of tires, the wails of a siren –

He never saw his boy's smile again.

Ever since that day, he would stop by toy shops to stare at the windows. If only he had enough money, maybe things would be different.

He saw children beaming, entering with their parents, leaving with an armful of bags and boxes.

Ah, he loved children. Their smiles were so pure, so precious. Every child deserved to smile.

He missed his boy. His beloved boy. He couldn't keep him smiling.

Maybe, maybe if he owned a toy store, he could keep their smiles –

The Heart Shop granted him a haven – the toy shop. A temptation, a mouse trap, a one-way trip with no exit. A place where children were forced to smile. He was technically getting what he wanted.

Rin felt her anger rising. She couldn't tell if it was more towards Mr. Nim, whose Desire had been twisted, or the Seed for manipulating the desire.

She turned to leave. Another moment longer, the emporium would be in flames.

At the entrance, Mr. Nim said, "Are you leaving already? Have you had enough fun?"

Fun? Who are you to decide whether I have enough fun?

"I'm not one of yours. You can't stop me," she said coldly.

The shop owner quietly retreated into his shop.

The hatred she had for the emporium made the tips of her fingers itch. Her flames were raging to be released, to burn the prison down, but she reminded herself that this was not his Territory. He was not the actual Master. He was only one of the many who fell for the Heart Shop's schemes, swept away by the delusions created by the Seed. A wrong move might destroy everything, including the photographs of the trapped children.

She decided to leave it alone for the time being.

Glancing down at the rest of the articles in her hands, she moved the missing children one to the back. The rest had headlines depicting unprecedented violence, thievery, assault, murder – all committed in unconceivable ways by the most unlikely people.

"Here, missy. Would you like some jerky?"

She turned around. A big man with a jolly round face that spelled enthusiasm was holding a plate of freshly cured jerky in her face.

Taking a step back and holding up a hand, she said, "No, I-"

"No need to be shy! The samples are on the house – satisfaction guaranteed. My jerky is the best in town! Look over there!" He jerked his head over at the long queue in front of a shop two lots away. "Customers can't get enough of them."

He led her towards his shop, blabbering about how good his jerky supposedly was.

I did not give away my heart for nothing. Now everyone knows of my shop.

The smell hit her the moment she heard the owner's Desire. Strong, raw, and metallic – it reminded her of the slaughterhouse near a wet market she once visited.

At the counter, she caught a glimpse of what looked like suspicious wet reddish mounds. The customers were leaving with paper bags that were dripping wet on the bottom, leaving a trail of dark droplets behind them.

And what did she just see through the transparent refrigerator door? She tore her eyes away and headed in the other direction before the owner could stop her.

She recalled one of the papers she read earlier – a feud between competing business owners along the street that ended in a bloody affair. It was an unpleasant thought, considering the circumstances, despite knowing that the Territory twisted reality based on its interpretation.

She couldn't tell how much of it was real. It was a well-known rule that within a Territory, it was advisable to take everything as it was and let it slide. The main priority was to find the Seed.

The problem was she simply couldn't find the way to the alley where it was.

The roads kept taking her back to the same spot, but the shop simply refused to be found.

The street clamored around her. She witnessed pots falling from above, a man clutching his heart and collapsing in the middle of the road, and a gambling house papered with money. She asked a handful of people about the Heart Shop, but none of them seemed to know what she was talking about.

The whispers of traded hearts hissed all around her, filling her ears, merging into incomprehensible sound.

I want to be famous.

I want to be a millionaire.

I hate him. He betrayed me. I want him dead.

Who are you to deserve happiness when you stole mine?

You scumbag! This is what you get for cheating on me!

She felt like she was walking in someone else's dream, multiple dreams that congregated in the same place. The strangeness was rubbing off on her. This was why Hunters usually worked in teams – so that they could keep each other sane.

"Don't you have a desire you would die for?"

The speaker was a man wearing a ragged two-piece. He was unkempt and barefooted. His facial hair was so thick that it nearly obscured his eyes. Like an additional piece of jigsaw that did not belong, he sat by the pavement as the world moved around him.

"Everyone has one. You – what is yours?"

Her head throbbed.

From the corner of her eyes, she saw a red-headed figure passing her by again.

She refused to look. She was not going to fall for the same trick twice.

Reveal your desire.

The lights were becoming disturbing. They were too bright, too many, too flashy.

She wondered if it was her or the Territory.

The man started to morph. One eye was becoming bigger than the other, his mouth crooked, his teeth magnified.

She heard a voice inside her head: *Why won't you let me look inside your heart?*

A female voice pulled her out of the illusion.

"Hey, missy, I see that you've been wandering about. Is there anything that catches your fancy?"

Her heart pounded as she looked around. The man was gone.

She had let her guard down – and the Seed took advantage of it.

"Hey, missy, over here."

It was one of the ladies from the gambling house. She wore a glittering navy-blue dress that reminded Rin of the Milky Way. Her eyeliner and mascara were so thick that they nearly merged with her brows. A satin ribbon sat atop her head like a crown.

Still not completely recovered from the experience earlier, Rin half-heartedly said, "I'm looking for the Heart Shop. You don't know anything about it, do you?"

The lady made a face. "The Heart Shop? Is it some kind of fad?"

"Whatever you're looking for, just make sure you avoid going down there." Another lady appeared, similarly dressed. She jerked her head towards the end of the street.

"Why?"

"Between you and me, it's not a good place."

"And why is that?"

The lady tutted in displeasure, as though unwilling to impart the words from her mouth but felt obligated to because Rin had asked. "Because someone died there."

"Oh, you mean the young couple who lived in that apartment?" The first lady lowered her voice. "I heard the poor girl was frightened to madness and took her own life. How tragic. They were going to get married..."

"I heard it was the man's ex-girlfriend who committed the unspeakable deed. How evil of her. She disappeared right after that."

"It was so scary how they ended up... I couldn't sleep that night when I heard."

Rin was certain the street held more bloody history than what was let on.

There was an unspoken rule when trapped within a Territory: following the hints would be the best lead to the Seed itself.

And it had been dropping obvious hints.

At least, it was better than waiting and doing nothing.

She headed in the direction they mentioned.

CHAPTER SIXTEEN

The apartment complex was cleverly hidden out of sight behind the main street. It was a set of old buildings with a quarter of its life worn down by the changing seasons and fickle weather. The walls were plastered with moss and grime. Rubbish piled up in the yard. Flies buzzed around the leftovers from a split bag. The gloom was a blemish to the image of Osmanthus Street – like a shameful childhood secret a rising star wanted to hide from the lenses of the public.

The iron gates were half-eaten by rust, scraping the gravel as Rin pushed past them. Barely any lights were on, or perhaps the windows were too cloudy to let any light through. She made her way up the nearest stairs, turning on the flashlight on her phone to illuminate the way. Deep cracks ran down the walls, and weeds grew along the stairwell. This place was long overdue for maintenance.

It wasn't too difficult looking for the unit people had spoken of earlier. It was barricaded by police tape and a large cardboard sign that read, *Danger! Keep out!*

Rin wondered if it referred to the Seed hiding inside or the possibility of encountering spirits of the deceased haunting the walls.

The door opened easily. Outlines of furniture greeted her. Lifting the tape at the door, she made her way in. The lights refused to turn on when she pressed the switch.

Under the flashlight, the living room was relatively untouched. A double couch with a set of matching cushions and leg rest. A round carpet in the middle of the floor, and a small television fixed to the wall. On the shelves sat several knickknacks: a miniature model of a clock tower, some mini car models, a ceramic teddy holding an empty basket, a snow globe, and a framed photograph of a happy couple on vacation.

It grew darker as she made her way inside. Rin felt her skin prickling, and she doubted it was solely because of the apparent drop in temperature. She couldn't help feeling watched. Grudges and malice remained, lurking like lost souls in the hallways. Deep claw marks traveled the entire length of the walls. Slightly below it was a trail of bloody palm stains and splatters of blood that ended in the kitchen.

The unsettling feeling grew stronger as she approached the bedroom.

It was a scene from a horror movie.

Blotches of blood filled her vision like carelessly thrown paint over the walls and furniture.

Torn sheets and a ripped mattress, glass shards from a mirror, overturned chairs, and a broken nightstand. A sole photograph lay among the pillow feathers.

It would be wise not to touch anything in a recent Territory bare-handed, especially in one where the enmity was still fresh. Summoning a small knife into her hand, she prodded at the photograph until she could see it properly.

A smiling couple waving at the camera, their faces blurred by bloodstains. Flipping it over, she saw a message written in frenzied strokes: *If I cannot have him, no one else can.*

A flash of someone else's memories.

"You promise, right? We'll always be together."

A teenage couple going out on a date.

A young lady calling someone over the phone – only to be greeted by voicemail.

An arguing couple.

"How could you? How could you marry her? How could you break the promise you made to me?"

"No, no, no, I shall make you mine."

The thoughts grew darker.

An exchange of a Sygn over a familiar piece of paper.

His sleeping face, so peaceful, smeared with blood. The smell of his blood so delicious – no, stop –

Her frightened face and her soundless scream –

"You!"

A blind red rage.

"If I cannot have you, no one else can."

Rin could feel the mercilessness of invisible fingers reaching for the back of her neck, closer, closer, seizing her –

Out of impulse, she raised her hand, plunging the blade into the photograph. The words vanished into thin air, and the photograph began to disintegrate.

Her heart pounded against her ribs. The memories and emotions shook her.

Rin always considered herself well-versed in Hunting, with five years of experience under her belt, but the Territory was making her question herself.

A Seed that granted the wishes of the masses. A Territory that stored Pulses that were not its Master's.

The thing she saw in the Pulse was definitely a Seed – most definitely the owner of the Pulse. Out of jealousy and anger at his betrayal, she became a Seed to seek revenge. Did it mean that the Heart Shop *gave* her the Seed in exchange for her heart?

Was that even possible? Why would the Heart Shop do such a thing?

The moment she left the unit, the weight lifted off her shoulders. It made her realize how tense she had been in there.

The sky was darker than before, a flat gray blue that seemed artificial. She could see Osmanthus Street with its glittering neon signs and floating lanterns from the corridor. The blaring music and amplified announcements now sounded obnoxious to her ears.

The clock struck three. The lights blew out one by one, and the streets descended into darkness. The music died down and within seconds, the town fell asleep.

Rin was the only person left wide awake in this strange place. Her mind wheeled, trying to connect everything she had seen, felt, and heard while in search of another clue.

She wanted to scream her frustrations out. Gripping the banister, she inhaled.

In, out, in, out –

Something moved down below. She leaned over the railing to get a better look.

Nothing. Nobody.

She blinked. Was it her imagination, or were the shadows growing in length?

A chill crept up her spine. Her shoulders tensed. Were the shadows...moving within themselves?

A pattering of footsteps caught her attention.

A figure was running as fast as he could across the courtyard, looking behind his shoulder as he did. Whoever it was, he was whimpering and sobbing in terror.

Behind him came another figure. Familiar.

Rin broke into a run, sprinting down the stairs across the courtyard.

There was no one in sight. For a moment, she thought she lost them.

A scream ripped the darkness apart. Shrill and unrelenting, echoing against the walls. No one seemed to hear him except Rin.

She knew she was heading the right way because the Seed's presence intensified.

A balding middle-aged man was slumped against the wall, legs jerking and fingers scraping uselessly against the ground. He was trying to speak, but instead of words, all that came out were gagging sounds. The whites of his eyes were alarmingly disproportionate to the black of his pupils.

Crouched in front of him was Hayle Signon, his jaw moving as though he was chewing. Tendrils connected whatever was inside his mouth to the red mud-like substance in his hand to the glowing shape of a heart visible on the man's chest.

"Hayle!"

He turned around, still eating – unconcerned by the state of the man in front of him.

The man saw her and tried to reach out a shuddering hand. The red heart faded to black, melting into a puddle of viscous gel that Hayle let slip between his fingers. The man let out a rattling gasp, eyes rolling backward, and went still.

"What are you doing?" It was a rhetorical question. Rin already knew the answer.

Hayle wiped his mouth and stood up. "Collecting debt."

She knew who he was doing it for.

For a moment, she wondered if this was how the Heart Shop was going to collect hers.

Standing in front of her was Hayle, yet not Hayle. The younger Signon twin was lively, kind, and too innocent for his own good. This person in front of her was cold, distant, and ruthless.

An unsettling feeling hovered in her gut. She wasn't a big fan of the Signon twins, but she did not like the idea of his awareness being trapped somewhere in the crevices of the Seed as it committed the unthinkable with his body.

He turned around to leave.

"Hayle!"

Rayve pounded towards them, skidded to a stop next to his brother, and caught his arm. Between ragged breaths and heaving shoulders, he said, "Hayle, I've been looking for you."

Hayle glanced at his twin, no hint of recognition and warm welcome in his eyes. Brushing Rayve's hand away, he said, "I have no business with you."

He left Rayve rooted to the spot and within a few seconds, he vanished into the shadows.

CHAPTER SEVENTEEN

Rayve sank onto the ground and buried his face in his hands.

"He will never forgive me," he mumbled to himself. "He'll never forgive me."

A child's screams, a sound of fear and despair and loud crashing as the roof overhead caved in –

Rin did not want to give him time to feel sorry for himself. "Where did you go?"

His head jerked up. "What do you mean? I'm supposed to ask you that question. Where did *you* go?"

Rin's stony silence gave him the answer.

"I was just standing there. It suddenly became night, and you were gone!" He waved his hand, returning to his usual irritable self. "I just kept walking and walking and ended up in the same place all the time. There was no way –" He stopped when he saw her expression.

She folded her arms. "Don't you think you owe me an explanation?"

Rayve seemed to struggle with himself for a moment. Rin could practically see his pride and helplessness waging war with each other. Then, pride gave in, and he said, "Fine. I'll talk."

*

When the twins were born on the thirteenth night of the moon cycle, the village labeled them as a pair of misfortunes.

When they were three, their family was forced to move to a house at the edge of the village as an excuse to spare most of the town from their inauspicious aura.

When they were four, Hayle found their father sleeping at the door, holding an ax in one hand.

When they were five, some villagers tried to throw them into the river.

When they were six, their village was attacked by a Seed.

They lost their parents and their home. Rayve nearly lost his last remaining family member.

As though the destruction of houses was insufficient to satiate the ravenous Seed, it turned its attention towards the helpless twins, picking one of them between its claws and preparing to devour him.

Six-year-old Rayve begged the heavens and anyone, anything that could hear his pleas to save his brother. By some miracle, the rubble above crashed onto the Seed, and in its moment of distraction, released its grip on Hayle.

Rayve did not look back. He grabbed Hayle and fled.

But the Seed's ability took a toll on Hayle, making him ill.

The survivors of the massacre did not look kindly at the twins. Doomed, the Seed must be their retribution – yes, it had to be them!

One day, under the temporary shelter set up for refugees, with Hayle sleeping next to him, Rayve heard the villagers talking behind their backs.

"They not only cursed their parents; they took everyone down with them. What little horrors," someone lamented.

"They should just die." The voice dripped with venom.

"We would be better off without them."

"Shh... What if they hear you? You'll be cursed!" a frightened voice squeaked.

Something inside Rayve broke.

"Shut up!" he screamed. The townspeople jumped back as though he carried a contagious disease. Hayle startled awake. "Go away!"

A rock hit him on the head. A hot trickle ran down the side of his face.

"Rayve!" Hayle clutched at his shirt. He started to cry. "Don't –"

"How dare you scream at us, little devil?" Someone bent down to pick up another rock. "You – your existence killed our kin! Aren't you monsters?"

"No one is going to protect you now, monsters! Serves you right!"

The older twin turned around and protected his younger brother as they were pelted with rocks.

On the same day, they were driven out of town armed with nothing but the clothes they had on their backs.

*

The filthy alleys were home to many: those who lost everything to failed investments, those who were kicked out of their homes, and those who had no one to take them in. To these people, the main street was the outside world, the place that had shunned them, the place they lost their footing in.

Every morning, the street burst to life with people going to work. They walked, drove, ran, and cycled. They moved. The inhabitants of the alley got ready to go to work as well. Getting ready involved walking out into the hostile outside world and picking a spot, waiting for coins to drop at their feet. It did not matter whether it was out of disdain or sympathy. All that mattered was that they would not have to go to bed with growling stomachs.

The people of the outside world mostly ignored them; beggars were merely eyesores that were better off unnoticed. Every day was the same. Even beggars had a routine - a routine to stay alive.

The spot beneath the rusty staircase of an abandoned shop was the home to a pair of twins. It was not exactly the best one, but at least it provided a little shelter from the rain.

Dying because of starvation and the bitter cold of the winters was a norm in the alleys. The cruelty of life did not matter. If someone was sick and starving and was unable to go out to earn some money, it was their business.

In this cruel world, there was only themselves and no space for anyone else.

Rayve grew up hating humans. He only saw them as self-entitled beings who were sources of money and food. He learned to recognize who to beg from – the kind elderly ladies, the pious rich who would give themselves a pat on the back after an act of philanthropy. He learned to pickpocket from the oblivious office-goers, teens hanging around with their friends, too busy talking to realize a light bump on their shoulder and a careful sleight of hand. Living off the streets hammered into him the fact that human hearts could be as filthy as the uncleaned chimneys at the tiny houses at the other end of town. He also learned that human lives could be as melodramatic as the shows he watched through the glass windows of the electronic store opposite his usual spot.

Gazes of contempt, lovers' spats, betrayals, hushed discussions behind the signboards, quick and illegal exchanges in the shadows of the alleys – he saw plenty, but bothered with none.

His exploits earned them enough food to get by and money for medicine whenever Hayle got sick. The winters were especially bad, with ruthless chills and increased Seed sightings. Hayle had grown very sensitive to the presence of Seeds ever since the incident, and going near Seeds would contribute to the relapse of his unknown disease.

Rayve eventually got them shelter in one of the quieter alleys at the back of the town. Hayle managed to find blankets from the nearby dumpster, some used clothes, a very useful electric cooker, and a not-so-useful small cupboard with a broken leg.

Hayle, being the kind soul he was, to Rayve's chagrin, would leave crumbs and leftovers of their hard-earned food for the strays outside to munch on. While Rayve learned how to live off the streets, Hayle seemed to have earned a self-taught skill on how to win arguments against him.

"They are as homeless as we were. Don't you feel sorry looking at them?" Hayle said that one time Rayve caught him putting out slices of cured meat for a stray dog that lost one of its hind legs in a scuffle.

And he would put on the most piteous look in his eyes that rendered Rayve speechless.

But he let it be. Because if one of them had to retain their humility, it would be Hayle.

They got through several seasons, but the second winter was when it all changed.

In that particular alley, they were not the only inhabitants. Rayve had always known the beggars that shared the same alley as them had always been keeping an eye on them – envious of their warmth and food, but they had always kept their distance.

One winter day, Hayle had been unwell. Rayve left him, promising to bring home enough money to buy some medicine and cook him something hot.

When he was away, the beggars came knocking at the door, begging Hayle to let them stay because one of them was very ill. Kind, good-willed Hayle let them in.

When Rayve returned, he found Hayle knocked unconscious outside their door and their 'home' taken over by the beggars. Alone against a group of full-fledged adults who would do anything to defend their newfound nest, he was no match for them.

Left out in the cold and with no money with them, Rayve carried Hayle to the nearest clinic only to be turned down.

Hours turned into days, and Hayle grew increasingly weak. Huddled together for warmth, Rayve desperately tried to shield his twin from the wind, all while trying to ignore the rumbling in his stomach.

"Don't die on me, Hayle," he whispered to his twin, whose body shuddered from the cold.

Please don't leave me alone, *he thought.* You're all that I have.

The world had abandoned them – no, they had been abandoned from the start. Why were they even born to begin with?

Were humans born to suffer and die? How unjust.

Rayve was so cold he couldn't feel his hands and feet anymore.

Maybe being a Seed would be a great idea. Then, he could devour all those who made them miserable. Curse the world, *he thought.* Curse it all...

"What are you two doing out in the cold like this?" a voice asked, sounding very far away. "You're going to die, you know."

Yes, and what does it matter to you? *Rayve thought to himself, barely having any energy to speak the words aloud.*

There was a small sigh, and the voice said, "Never mind. You're coming with me."

There was a slight tug as someone lifted Hayle.

Rayve retaliated. No one was taking Hayle away from him.

Between the crack of his half-opened eyes, he saw a middle-aged man, no older than his father, peering at him – one hand on Hayle's arm, wearing a bemused expression, curious eyes behind his oval glasses.

"Your brother is dying, little guy. And you are too unless you come with me," he said. "Don't glare at me like that. I'm not a witch that eats children, you know."

The man carried Hayle up in his arms and turned to Rayve. "Are you coming or not?"

He was a Council officer, and he gave them what nobody had ever offered the twins.

In front of a warm fire within proper brick walls, shielded from the blizzard outside, Hayle safely tucked in bed after taking medicine, Rayve finally came to terms with knowing that man had saved them. He had forgotten what it felt like to take a hot bath, wear clean clothes, eat freshly made food, and sleep in a proper bed.

And most importantly, that man saved Hayle.

Rayve was standing on a breaking cliff – jumping or falling would make no difference, and that man was all the difference he needed.

The man, who would then become their mentor, was light brighter than the sun itself – their ray of hope and their ultimate savior, and Rayve vowed to repay him in any way possible.

CHAPTER EIGHTEEN

Rin, who listened in silence, finally said, "Knowing that Hayle is susceptible to Seeds and getting injured means he would heal slower, yet he makes you both Hunters. Doesn't that count towards using you?"

She knew who their mentor was.

Baltory Weis. The Section Head of the Division of Internal Investigations, Department of Law Enforcement.

Cnaris hated his guts. Rin didn't like him either. She found him too much pretense and too little substance.

Rayve turned away. "You don't understand. Even if he does, it doesn't matter. I will do anything for him." He clenched his fists. "And I'll protect Hayle too."

The older Signon twin turned out to be someone who threw in everything in a gamble. She wondered if his actions were more parts bold or more parts stupid.

You'll lose it all in one wrong move, she thought to herself, *and already very close to it too.*

"So, you decided to trade your heart?" she asked.

"I...I went ahead of myself," he forced himself to concede. "I heard about the Heart Shop – that they offered anything in return for some kind of payment."

"So you asked them to cure Hayle?"

"Yes," Rayve hissed through his teeth. "I told them I was willing to pay, but they lied to me. They held Hayle captive."

Rin did not want to ask what he paid them with. She thought the contract was full of loopholes to begin with. The biggest loophole was the unknown nature of the Seed.

"Making him part of the Seed removed his weakness" Rin said They didn't lie. You were the one who took the bait."

"They did. It made his condition worse than before."

"No," Rin said firmly. "When he becomes a Seed, he will no longer have the problem."

Rayve's eyes widened in horror. "He is not going to become a Seed."

"You're not the one having the last say, not after selling your brother to the shop." The words came out before she could help herself. Rayve turned whiter than a sheet. "I told you to stop before you regret it."

"Thank you for reminding me, and this is precisely why I came to you for help," Rayve said, tone rising in anger.

"So you're hiring me?"

"I'll pay you if you ask for it-" he snapped and stopped, realizing how foolish he sounded. "Darn it all! Are you enjoying yourself now?"

"No, I'd rather be in bed, rather than getting stuck in other people's lives and stories – all of which have nothing to do with me."

"Well, you're stuck here with me now. Do you have a way out of it?"

Rin turned on the spot, examining her surroundings. The night was unnaturally silent and incomplete. She wondered if the Master was watching somewhere. "The rules were created by the Master himself. This Territory belongs to a Seed, and there's ultimately only one way to handle a Seed."

"How are you going to –" Rayve began and stopped as realization dawned on him.

She gave him a cold smile. "When it comes down to it, I'm going to destroy it all – this pretentious clockwork street, and the Heart Shop along with it."

CHAPTER NINETEEN

Rin was surprised when Rayve found the way to the Heart Shop almost effortlessly. The alleys twisted and turned like a maze threatening to swallow them, but Rayve navigated the route with the certainty of a regular.

A feeble light flickered behind the glass doors. The signage above creaked as it swung back and forth.

She stared at the steps leading down to the entrance and asked, "How did you do it?"

Rayve, with his fists clenched and face lined with determination, said, "Who cares? We're here."

He made his way down the stairs and barged through the doors. The bell tinkled, the sound reverberating into the distance.

"Hayle!" His voice was loud and rude enough to wake slumbering things that ought to keep slumbering. Rin had the impulse to shut him up.

At the center were metal bars that traversed the entire height of the shop. Behind the bars stood a table, illuminated by a small hanging red lightbulb they could see from the outside.

The signboard let out a long, weary whine.

Sitting very still and empty-eyed, skin dyed reddish by the light that cast shadows over his features, the prisoner within the cage was Hayle.

"Hayle!" Rayve crossed the room, grabbed the bars, and shook them. "Wake up! Come to your senses!"

The back of Rin's neck prickled. The signboard creaked again.

"Hayle! Look at me!"

Almost instinctively, Rin's eyes traveled upwards to the dense shadows above them.

"Hey," she warned, not looking away. "We've got company."

A burst of malice erupted from above, like an invisible hand prying Rayve away from the bars, followed by an ear-splitting cry that sounded like the sound of a gate that was in dire need of oiling. Rayve rolled over onto all fours, cushioning his fall.

The Seed took the form of a corrugated sphere with a single eye in the middle. It towered over them. Tendrils hung from it, extending down to Hayle's body, draping themselves around his arms almost possessively.

Hayle's eyes flickered shut, and he keeled over.

Rayve's eyes glinted with fury. "You scum!"

He charged forward. Using the table as leverage, he leaped into the air and charged the Seed with a magnetic field.

Rin drew out her throwing knives.

"Stay out of it, Elziel!" Rayve snarled. "It's mine!"

Repelled by the Seed's magnetic field, the metal bars blew apart, sending shards flying outwards. On the verge of hitting the ground, they stopped, spun like a needle on a compass, and flew towards it.

The splinters skewered the Seed, sharp ends piercing through its thin surface.

"How *dare* you touch him?"

The small weapons tore and hacked at the tendrils with each word. One after another, they broke free from Hayle. The Seed reeled, the eyeball rolling upwards on itself.

Rayve darted around it, manipulating the fields. The Seed bulged and ballooned, making strangled sounds, the remnants of its tendrils wasted on the ground.

Rin watched, a frown forming between her brows. It was rare to see a Seed that hardly retaliated.

"Wait, this is –"

The eye shuddered violently. Rin barely had time to shield herself as the Seed broke apart. Dust showered onto them, most of it falling onto Hayle.

Coughing as she accidentally inhaled some of it, she thought she heard a distant wail – a faraway siren distorted onto itself like a dying radio.

Silence.

For a moment, Rin found herself standing in darkness – cold, chilling, and alive.

Then, the stillness broke, and the Territory rippled. A loud, drawn-out cry reverberated throughout the space, like an infant throwing a tantrum after being woken up from sleep and robbed of its favorite toy.

Great, he had done it. She had meant to tell Rayve this was not the Seed they were after; this was probably just a part of its body. Destroying it seemed to have alerted the Seed, and now it was mad.

Rayve seized Hayle, hair and shoulders white with dust, hoisted him onto his shoulders, and turned to Rin. "What are you waiting for? Let's get out of here!"

*

"This has to be the place, right? I mean, it reeks." Edwin wrinkled his nose, staring at the invisible barrier of a Territory ahead of him.

The owner of the pickle store nearby heard him and scowled.

Moments after they arrived at the town of Pallin, they were greeted by a powerful Seed presence. Kazu glanced at the signboard next to them: *Osmanthus Street – all lights and soul of the evening.*

"Arr 'oo planning 'o visit 'ze famous street, young man?" an elderly man running the hardware shop opposite called out, flashing his missing front teeth. "Fraid 'oo arr 'oo early. 'Ze shops 'zere only opens after 'ze sun 'oes down."

"Not a good place, that street," the disagreeable-looking pickle seller said, barely looking up.

"You're only saying that because they robbed your business," a middle-aged lady carrying a basket of laundry chipped in scornfully as she walked past.

"I'm not!" the pickle seller snapped. "Look, you don't go around talking behind my back just because I refused to sell you my –"

"What do you mean, it's not a good place?" Kazu interrupted.

The man shrugged, scratching his stubble. "No one from here goes in there. And yet, every evening the streets just fill up with people."

There was a long silence.

"You're making it sound like a horror story!" The lady with the laundry gasped.

"I'm not making it up, woman! Look, my stall is right next to the entrance, and I'm open every day. Barely anyone passed by here, see?" The pickle seller flushed red as he spoke. "Unless they're invisible!"

Edwin leaned closer to Kazu and whispered, "Reckon he's quite right. Strange how the Council never found out about this place."

"They wouldn't if no one ever reported it," Kazu pointed out. The street ahead was empty, but he was certain it was a mirage created to fool outsiders. "Let's go."

"Hey!" the pickle seller called out. "You don't believe me?"

Edwin glanced over his shoulder. "Of course, we believe you, mister. That's the reason we're going in."

With a chuckle, he went after Kazu, leaving the flabbergasted man behind.

*

The Seed was enraged.

The ground distorted and undulated as they made their way along the tortuous alleys. Rin had no idea where they were going. Cries for help, wails of agony, and screams of fear filled her ears, painting imagery of a war-torn landscape, a disaster-split region, a tragedy-marred household. It was difficult to keep herself upright as the ground rocked and shifted.

Rayve was a short distance ahead of her, dodging a dislodged brick that threatened to split his skull while carrying Hayle on his back. Nearly tripping over loose stones, she gripped the pillars and walls as she followed him.

They ran and ran. The quaking, falling debris, and noise followed them tirelessly, drilling into her ears.

The alleys let up to the courtyard of the apartment earlier.

They were greeted by a horrible sight. The inhabitants were outside, rolling on the ground, clutching their heads and screaming incoherent words.

Losing its source of food, the Seed had turned on the people linked to its Territory.

Rin couldn't help wondering if their actual selves still existed, tormented by the Seed, or was this another part of a show put up by the Master?

A man staggered towards them, moaning, hands outstretched. Rayve sidestepped him, and he lurched forward, losing balance, and fell.

"Give me... Give...me..." Another man lumbered from the shadows, a kitchen knife glinting in his hand. "Give me your heart!" he roared and charged Rin.

She grabbed his hand and twisted. With a cry, the man dropped the knife, and she kicked his feet from underneath him, sending him falling face down.

"Help me..." The little girl she kept seeing stumbled towards her. She broke into a run, pouncing on Rin with surprising agility and strength, knocking her onto the ground.

"Elziel!" She barely heard Rayve's voice over the din.

A pair of cold, small hands wrapped themselves around her neck. "Help me," the girl begged. Behind the tears falling off her cheeks, she was smiling.

An expression of exhilaration.

Rin pushed her away, and the girl rolled across the pavement, clambering to her feet like it did not hurt in the least.

"Elziel!" Rayve said again. "Let's leave!"

The girl was making her way towards Rin again, still smiling. Rin opened her mouth –

Quiet.

The scene and the noises glitched like a malfunctioning videotape, and then suddenly, the lights flared up, and the streets became lively again.

The people who were shrieking in pain earlier got to their feet, put smiles on their faces, and hurried off towards the main street. The girl let out a delighted laugh and scampered away.

This was another form of madness.

The clockwork had malfunctioned.

Every time it happened and the way it did, Rin felt her sanity slip away by a margin.

"Elziel, hurry!" Rayve said. Hayle was still unconscious on his back. "We need to get him out of here as soon as possible."

She refused to move. Enough of being pulled and pushed around.

Every Hunter knew that escape was impossible and pointless when facing a rampaging Seed that was close to maturity. There was only one way to end it all, and it was to destroy the Seed's core once and for all.

It was clear that the street and its inhabitants were running out of time. Most of them had probably already expired. They were now standing on a ticking time bomb, and the gates were tightly barricaded.

Yet Rayve, he –

She had felt there was something off with him when she met him after encountering Hayle, and she could not place her finger on it. Was he pretending, or did he not realize it himself?

"You led me here." She said.

"Huh? What are you talking about?"

"You found the Heart Shop. You knew where you were going all the time, yet you led me here. You also knew the Seed that trapped Hayle is not the real thing. What are you trying to do?"

Rayve blinked, his eyebrows pinched together into a frown. "What do you mean? I'm trying to get us out of here! Hayle needs help."

"To help Hayle is to destroy the actual Seed, not to rile it up and then try to escape. You and I both know this very well."

Confusion flashed across his face. "I…"

"Why are you intentionally, or unintentionally, stalling? Exactly whose side are you on?"

Rayve opened and closed his mouth – but no words came.

"Oh, well, *they* just have to disturb me when I'm trying to sleep."

Lazy and lulling. Low and languid.

Rin and Rayve spun in the direction of the voice.

He was dressed like a townsperson: baggy clothes with not much consideration for style or color. A tomato stain adorned the front of his shirt. Tall, lanky, and slouching, his hair appeared to be the most neglected part of his body, unkempt like a fraying brush, hanging over his ears and nearly touching his shoulder. He squinted at them through drooping eyelids that seemed perpetually drowsy.

The back of Rin's neck prickled.

Not a single sound, not a hint of his presence, and suddenly, he was there. It was always the unassuming ones that were the most dangerous because they were easily overlooked and underestimated.

This man was a very dangerous person.

Rayve clearly sensed the concealed malice because his face drained of color.

"Who are you?" the stranger slurred, as though anything more would use up too much energy and he had very little to spare. "I don't remember you."

Neither Rin nor Rayve moved.

The man scratched his head and answered the question himself. "Ah, must be the Hunters they told me about." He let out a sound between a sigh and a groan. "How bothersome."

The air between them smoldered. A sharp killing intent but with nothing in sight.

"Who are you?" Rin finally asked. She realized her palms were damp. She was also suddenly aware of her heart pounding in her ears.

The man moved with surprising agility. One moment he was five feet from them, the next he was directly in front of Rayve. "This person. That person. Instructions. Orders. How troublesome." His eyes glazed over, and a bored, bothered look crossed his face. "Why does everyone want to disturb my nap?"

He peered into Rayve's white face as though he could find the answer.

"Heart," he muttered, words running over each other. "Trade heart. Wishes for heart. Heart. Him and the heart."

A crazed look took over his eyes. "*Are you reminding me that I don't have one?*"

He held his palm over Rayve's face.

Four fingers.

Rayve's eyes went wide as he stood frozen, lips half-parted in shock.

Rin's body reacted before her mind told her to. Pushing Rayve out of the way, she felt the stranger's hand come down on her shoulder, piercing through her skin like blades.

A sharp flash of pain shot through her senses as she flung a knife at him from close range.

He dodged it with ease and withdrew his hand, sending droplets of red flying.

She stumbled, dots flying across her vision, blood running down the length of her arm.

"Elziel!"

She glared at Rayve. "Do you have a death wish?"

What kind of speed did the man possess?

Rin was taught how to judge an opponent within the first five seconds of an encounter. She knew her limits. He was just standing there, flexing his neck, fingers smeared with her blood, and she knew that he was dangerously powerful, way above her capabilities.

He could kill them within a blink.

She realized that her question to Rayve was obsolete.

There was no way they could escape the man's pursuit.

Out of desperation than anything else, she flung two knives in his direction.

He dodged the first almost lazily, and the second nicked a strand of his hair.

Rayve took advantage of his momentary distraction to activate his ability. Rin's knives changed direction mid-air and whizzed straight toward the back of the man'shead.

The man tilted himself backward, and the blades hurtled an inch above his nose into the opposite wall.

The ground cracked beneath his feet, and the earth particles floated in response to Rayve's ability. The stranger vanished from the spot and reappeared next to Rayve, kicking him across the face.

Both the twins were thrown across the ground.

"Hayle…" Rayve reached for his brother.

The man stepped on his hand. There was a crack, and Rayve cried out in pain.

"Why won't you stop moving?" the man drawled. "Need to end this. Want to sleep."

Rin closed the distance between them, blade in her hands, aiming for his neck.

It happened so fast that she had no time to react.

A force knocked her into a wall, and she tasted blood on her lips. His hands closed around her neck, pinning her to the spot.

He had not even shifted his feet- Rayve's hand still trapped.

Rin had never felt so powerless.

Perhaps enticed by the scent of blood, the Seed lurking in the background began to move earnestly. In between the lines of her fading consciousness, she felt shadows emerging from the walls, wrapping themselves around her and dragging her in.

CHAPTER TWENTY

When Kazu entered the Territory, it presented itself to him in an unpretentious manner. It was reminiscent of the street he saw when he looked out of his window at home. Stalls lined the pavement, competing for the limelight. Shops selling various goods that fulfilled both needs and wants of the people. The only thing it was missing was the canal that ran right through the town of Creave.

He ambled down the street, looking around with mild interest. A clothing store with a mannequin facing backward. A restaurant serving rice on golden plates. A toy store that appeared ten times bigger inside than on the outside.

Interesting.

This was what dreamlike felt like. Dreams were often incohesive, strange, and lacking logic. The same applied to Territories.

The difference was awareness. Territories retained awareness; dreams did not.

A small figure bumped into him. Grabbing his arm, she cried, "Help me!"

It was a girl, around ten or so. Her white dress was ragged and smudged with dirt. Her shoulder-length hair was unruly and plastered all over her face. She appeared to have been running. Her bare feet were blistered and sore.

"What happened?" His eyes found a bruise purpling over her jaw.

A sob escaped her. "My father hit me. I ran from home. He will come for me." She grabbed his arm and glanced behind her fearfully. "Please help me."

No one else along the street seemed to be surprised by her appearance. They did not even seem to *notice* her.

Kazu gently removed her hand and said, "I'm here to look for someone. Have you by chance seen her?"

She did not answer immediately. Instead, she bowed her head and said in a piteous voice, "Mister..."

Kazu drew out his gun and pointed it at her. "I think you should be more careful choosing who to speak to."

The girl lifted her head slowly. The disguise peeled off. She was no longer wearing the smudgy white dress but a proper black shirt-dress and a pair of black tights. Her black hair was smooth and tidy, resting comfortably above her shoulders, its tips clinging to her chin. A pair of high-heeled boots covered her feet right up to her knees.

The barrel of his gun aligned directly over the spot between her cold, gray eyes.

In a flat tone, she said, "You're the first person to see through my illusion."

Kazu smiled in acknowledgment.

A tinkling laugh came from his right, and another girl appeared. She was about Rin's age, dressed in a white blouse and matching checkered skirt and tie. Her waist-long bubblegum pink hair was a graceful cascade down her back. A small red crescent piercing winked from the corner of her left eye.

She removed a bright pink lollipop from between her teeth and waved it at him. "I like you." She rounded on him, flashed a pair of pointed molars, and blew a puff of raspberry-smelling breath in his face. "So fine, so handsome. Best of all, you outwitted Cecila."

His body reacted the moment the corner of his eyes caught a twitch of movement.

A deep gash etched the ground where he had been standing a moment ago. The older girl whistled, lowering her hand.

"Sweet! I like you even more now." She winked at him. "Name is Jessabelle. Jess or Jessie – whichever you like."

"Jessie!" the girl called Cecila snapped. "I thought you're supposed to be with Master."

"Master? Naaaw, he doesn't need me around him," Jessabelle drawled. "He's probably sleeping somewhere."

"Precisely why he needs someone with him! We have important work to do!"

"Work, work, work. That's all you talk about. What a bore."

Cecila scowled.

"I'm sorry, but *who* are you?" Kazu interrupted.

The girls' attention turned to him.

For the first time, Cecila's lips curved upwards into a small smile. she spoke with a hint of pride. "I suppose you will find out sooner or later. We belong to an organization known as the King's League. Our role is to supervise the growth of the Seed. We are both Quantum's retainers, even though" – a haughty expression crossed her face – "I'm the one doing the work most of the time."

Whoever Quantum was, he was not the Seed's Master.

Kazu found himself struggling to connect the dots. To begin with, he was like a last-minute substitute for a match where everyone else had ample time to prepare and had to rely on superficial information obtained from an online forum.

"So," he began slowly, "the Heart Shop is your doing?"

"Yes and no," Cecila said. "I told you. We are, ah, what you humans call observers. But of course, the Seed must come from somewhere."

"Ta-da! We are the ones who gave this precious Seed to him!" Jessabelle exclaimed. "Because he was so desperate for it."

The entire street was now empty except for the three of them, its illusion worn-out.

"He?" Kazu asked quietly.

"The Manager. The one who runs the Heart Shop. Do you believe a Seed has the ability to grant every wish? Do you really believe a Seed is capable of equivalent trade?" Cecila smiled coldly.

"What do you mean?"

"We played the role of Santa Claus. We gave them presents!" Jessabelle hopped onto a fire hydrant, balancing herself on top of it. "Hey, Ceci, are we about done? This place is boring. It's party and sleep and party and sleep over and over. Let's finish up and go home."

"If you'd slacked off less and gotten a Hunter's heart sooner, then we would be done by now."

"Hey, one just came marching right up to him a couple of weeks ago. That maroon ponytail guy – I think he has a twin." Jessabelle looked excited. "Do you think he sold off his twin's heart?"

Kazu frowned. "You seem very excited about the prospect."

"Of course! See, a Hunter's heart helps the Seed grow bigger and bigger." She waved her hands above her head, nearly falling off her perch. "And there are so, so many Hunters around today!"

"Excuse me, but why a Hunter's heart?"

"Which do you think appeals more to the Seed? If you are given a chance to feast on a king's platter after an entire year of dry bread, what would you do? Tainted hearts are like dry bread. The people here had their hearts stained by their selfishness and greed. How do you think a Seed would feel if they encountered a Hunter's tempered heart?"

Kazu felt rather out of place, listening to a mysterious girl giving him a lecture on a Seed within a Territory.

"This place was doomed from the start." Cecila carefully tucked a loose strand of hair behind her ears. "Stupidity and greed have something in common: they are highly contagious. When the people saw that trading hearts brought wealth, they started doing it too. It didn't take long before they started using it as a means of satisfying their grudges and products of envy without dirtying their own hands. None of them realized they were building a path towards their own destruction. Do you know within this street itself, how many of their kind humans have killed out of selfishness?"

He understood what she implied. Seeds affected everyone in their Territory. The more you fed it, the more it gave in return. The more hearts it fed on, the stronger the Seed became, and the more tempted people became. It was a vicious cycle that would ultimately bring detriment to those under its prolonged influence.

Jessabelle was humming a tune that was reminiscent of "Mulberry Bush" while spinning.

Cecila ignored the interruption. "Such foolishness. All they saw were the gains, and for the gains, it's all right to forsake others. In other words, it's the weak minds of humans that lead to their downfall."

She eyed him, gouging his reaction. "Interesting. You don't seem to disagree."

"I don't agree either. I'm not planning to judge anyone," he said.

"Well, it doesn't matter whether you do. What does a person's opinion matter anyway? An excited Seed feeds more than usual. In other words, your presence as Hunters facilitates its growth-"

A thought struck him. "Did you, by chance, lead my friend here?"

Jessabelle laughed – high-pitched, amused.

Cecila smiled, pleased. "Very astute. Let's just say everything falls into place of its own."

They were right – the Seed was excited, very excited. He sensed it, an unsettling presence crawling through the grounds, climbing up the walls, hiding in the crevices of the alleys, impatient roots crawling up to him.

As they spoke, it was expanding, blooming like an ugly flower, reaching toward the fake sky above their heads. The pressure pressed against him like a crowd in a commuter.

Both Cecila and Jessabelle were smirking. The girls had stalled enough time.

His ears were starting to buzz with illegible noises, like tuning a radio and getting multiple stations at that one overlapping frequency.

Kazu was not the type to panic when trapped in a sticky situation. He did not retaliate – not because it was too late, but at times, he just happened to prefer to go with the flow.

Sometimes, the harder you struggled, the tighter the ropes got.

"The way you speak of humans, it's as if you're not one yourself." He asked one final question as the Seed's tendrils crept around him, unseen but felt: "Exactly who are you?"

"I'll tell you since you're so eager for an answer." Cecila drew herself to her full height. "We witness, we observe, and we judge. We are everywhere. We are the people of Reverse-"

Buzzing filled his ears, louder and louder, nearly drowning out her next words.

"- and we are here on a mission. Someone has to retrieve Master Imp's creation."

*

When Edwin entered the Territory, it presented itself to him in an unpretentious manner. It reminded him of the street near his home, sparsely occupied by dull and lifeless shops, overlooking an old church no one went to. Overflowing bins rummaged by strays and cigarette butts half-buried in the ground. Dim lanterns swung overhead, suspended on dangerously thin and frail wires. The lighting was the unpleasant cool gray on an evening that was about to rain.

He hated it. He wondered if he had accidentally teleported elsewhere because his mind could not fathom how and why this street was popular.

Edwin stomached the distaste of his surroundings and strolled up to a stall selling skewers.

Or at least, he thought they were skewers.

They turned out to be plastic models of skewered meat, sausages, broccoli –

His stomach rumbled in protest. He had abandoned his lunch after receiving Rin's message. Sleep deprived and hungry, he let out a long sigh.

The people around him were moving as though programmed, unnaturally rigid, with one hand poised strategically behind their backs.

On closer look, they were all holding some form of weapon.

Great, he was about to witness a variety of weapons on display.

"The stupid cat owes me lunch and two days' worth of sleep," he muttered under his breath as he slid his hand into his coat pocket.

CHAPTER TWENTY-ONE

There was once a child who was always told the same thing.

"See," his father said, ripping a piece of bread between his teeth, "your life is worth less than a glass of beer."

The child hung his head.

The bruises on his arms stung, and his body ached – but not as much as the fragile heart of a seven-year-old.

No one told him otherwise. Not even his mother, who left him with his debt-ridden, gambler father.

His classmates always picked on him. His teachers never sided with him.

His father's debt collectors loved ambushing him on the way back from school.

He was always beaten up.

No one cared.

And no one ever would.

*

Rin woke up on top of a clockwork to the sound of soft piano music. It was a slow and simple melody, lacking intent or flourish.

Her body ached, and her wrists were bound behind her. She struggled to sit up, wincing as her shoulder gave a nasty throb.

Beneath the transparent floor was a giant set of revolving gears and mechanisms of unfathomable complexity.

A short distance away, a couple waltzed across the floor. The
man, with his brunette hair slicked back, wore a dress coat
adorned with a red rose over his chest pocket. His polished shoes
shone as bright as Cnaris' prided glassware collection. The lady
was a delicate beauty with oval eyes, small, peach-colored lips,
and elegant golden braids that fell down her back. Her layered
dress trailed across the floor as she spun and twirled to the music.
Flecks of white cascaded around them like fresh snow.
Illuminated by the spotlight from above, the sight was ethereal.

Further behind was a grand piano in all its splendor. Lying motionless near the piano stool was Hayle. The person playing it was –

Kazu.

The shock of the realization was like electricity pulsing through her skin. *Why is he here?*

Did he come because of her message? Was he real, or was he a trick – a product of the Territory?

The flat melody hammered into her a sense of foreboding.

Rin was very familiar with Kazu's music. A long time ago, she requested that he compile it into a playlist so that she could listen to it whenever she wanted to. His music spoke emotions, pictured the weather, and told a story – light like clouds sailing through the sky on a clear day, tranquil like morning dew clinging to the tips of leaves, angry like turbulent skies before a downpour.

This sounded like a machine that lacked a soul, playing for the sake of producing sound.

The music picked up speed, and the dance steps became sharper, fancier. Head tossed back, arms flung out, arching backs, frantic feet tapping over the floor, it was a performance teetering on the brink of danger and lunacy.

Someone clapped. To her left, the man who demanded her heart earlier was applauding. The clapping grew louder and louder as more and more townspeople gathered around them. Soon, the couple was surrounded by a crowd, their applause sounding like a standing ovation at a concert hall.

At the final note, the couple ended their dance with a flourish.

The man bowed to his audience and waved. The lady, on the other hand, stood stiffly by his side with a passive expression.

"Thank you, esteemed guests." The man said, "Thank you for gracing us with your presence."

He was looking at her.

The audience vanished as suddenly as they appeared.

"I believe we have met before, young lady." He made his way towards her, wringing his gloved hands together.

"You're the Manager."

She had recognized his voice the moment he spoke – the soft, lilting tone of a salesperson that was well-versed in addressing concerns, promoting products, and convincing buyers.

He smiled at her approvingly. "That is correct."

She glanced over at Kazu. He was sitting very still at the piano, fingers poised over the black and white keys, eyes gazing at nothing. *Is he really Kazu?*

The Manager noticed. "Do not fret, young lady. I assure you he is in no state of suffering. I have been waiting for you ever since you came of your own volition. Never did I expect another Hunter to step in before you. Well, like they say, the more the merrier."

"What have you done to him?" Rin demanded, struggling to keep her voice level. She refused to let him know how she was feeling.

The Manager smiled like a teacher encouraging his pupil. "I just happened to look into his heart."

His lady companion blinked slowly. Rin had the strangest feeling that she was a moving doll.

"Did you happen to look into your companion's heart as well?" She asked, glancing at the lady.

The Manager chuckled. "Young lady, I cannot even if I wanted to." He stepped over to his beautiful partner and touched her face lightly. "Because she does not have one."

He paused for effect. "My dearest Emilia is a Creation."

A Creation – an artificial being spun from ancient forbidden magic. They resembled human beings but lacked everything that made them one. They were meant to serve as puppets in the rebel war that dated a couple of centuries back because of their lack of compassion and their nonexistent sense of pain. The Council had destroyed the manufacturing plants, incapacitated the ones involved, banned all information on Creations, and enacted a law that forbade further endeavors.

Rin never thought she would encounter one in person.

"I will give her a heart." The Manager clapped his hand over his chest.

Rin finally knew his true intention: to forge a heart from all that he got from the townspeople and give it to Emilia. "A heart isn't made up of a jumble of emotions and intentions you gather from others."

It was meant to be cultivated from experiences and strengthened by the values imparted from life lessons.

It was meant to leap with joy, weep with sorrow, tremble with anticipation, grovel with regret –

A heart had to know how to *feel.*

He had convinced himself – or had *been* convinced – that he could achieve the impossible.

"Then, how about you tell me, young lady?" He stepped closer to Rin. " I am curious what yours looks like."

He leaned down and tilted her chin up so that she was looking at him. She struggled against her binds, trying not to look into his eyes. His grip was surprisingly strong, and she wasn't feeling her best.

"Would you let me look into your heart?"

It was not a question. It was a perfunctory knock on the door to let the owner know he was going to enter with or without permission.

She found herself trapped within his gaze, unable to look away. The black of his eyes grew larger until they swallowed the golden irises, until they morphed into one and claimed the whole of his face.

It bloomed outwards, engulfing the edges of her vision.

She was standing in a warehouse. In front of her was a smoldering black Magic Circle. In the middle was a familiar bloodied, battered figure, held up by his wrists by invisible ropes.

Rei.

Five people stood around him, one of them turning a sword in his hand. Without warning, he stabbed Rei in the chest.

"Rei!"

He lifted his head. Blood dribbled down the corner of his mouth as he whispered, "Don't come."

The pain on his face pierced through her heart. Somewhere inside her, she knew she had seen this, been there before – but she could not look away.

Stop.

Her legs disobeyed her, taking one step and another towards him.

Stop.

His lips parted, saying something she couldn't hear. The figure next to him lifted the sword again, ready to strike –

No!

The image broke.

She was on her feet, disoriented and shaky. An arm caught her around the shoulders, and she glanced up.

Blonde hair, and the familiar nevus below his right eye.

Next to her was Kazu, his gun pointed at the Manager.

Relief washed through her – a wonderful, welcoming feeling. At that moment, she almost wanted to laugh.

The Manager's look of surprise was just as profound. "How?"

"I never said I'd let you look." Kazu said, his voice low.

Rin had never seen him so angry.

The Manager regarded him with interest. "What strong willpower. I am curious. Exactly what are you trying so hard to hide?"

Rin thought she saw something flash through Kazu's eyes. That moment passed, and she wondered if she had imagined it.

In a fluid movement, he cut her free from her binds. She had a dozen questions rushing through her mind, but no words came.

He noticed the questions in her eyes and responded with a look that said, *Later.*

Rin obliged.

Over at the piano, Hayle stirred.

"You lost," Rin said. "Give it up."

The Manager sighed. "Well, this is unexpected, but thankfully, I have prepared for such contingencies."

The back of Rin's neck crawled. The Seed stirred.

A thick, concentrated presence was rising, and it seemed to be coming from –

Below.

The mechanism clunked and tinkled with fervor.

The Manager smiled. "It turns out to be sufficient. We are just one step away from success."

Cracks formed in the transparent floor. The air stirred with unease, and the space started to shudder.

The Manager turned to Emilia and whispered, "Are you excited, my love?"

The walls fractured, pieces falling off and revealing the nothingness behind it.

An expression of alarm crossed Kazu's face. He glanced at Rin, and she knew he was thinking the same as her.

The Seed was ripping its Territory apart.

"Stop!"

Kazu's warning fell on deaf ears and a hardened, twisted will. Too late to turn back.

The Seed's aura was thick and suffocating. It was awakening, a snake uncoiling after months of hibernation, a parasitic flower blooming after absorbing the necessary nutrients – eager to feed, ready to devour.

The Master was serving himself up on the sacrificial plate.

"Emilia is my everything. She is the one who made me feel alive again. She is the only thing I have had throughout my life. I shall give it all back to her."

A powerful force broke forth from where he was standing, throwing them back. Rin's feet skidded over the floor, stopping only when she hit the wall. Looking up, pieces of the Territory rained down on them like confetti.

In the center of the stage, the Manager stood with Emilia next to him, as rigid and expressionless as before.

He embraced her. "Everything will be all right."

*

A man with empty eyes walked down the street on a drizzling evening. The sky, the buildings, and the asphalt were a dull gray, like his soul.

He had just finished his meager desk job for the day. He did not like it, but he could not hate it. He had no idea if he had ever had a dream. There was nothing else he could become. He was unqualified; his resume was blank. His presence was subservient. His employers only called after no one else wanted the spot.

His colleagues were advantage-seeking bastards with their hands rubbing, waist buckling, and flattering laughs, sucking up to their superiors for promotions.

He learned their ways – not for promotions, but to reduce unpaid overtime and additional work that was supposed to belong to someone else.

Today, he was lucky. He managed to get off work on time. Tomorrow, he would be back there again.

Day after day, the world seemed to lose color little by little. Someday, perhaps it would end up completely white or black.

Then, he caught sight of a pair of eyes just like his. Eyes that had no vision for the future.

They belonged to a girl. Crouching by a dumpster like an abandoned doll, she looked at her feet. Her long hair hung limply over her shoulders, dull and lifeless.

She was drenched. Her pale skin glistened in the rain. Raindrops clung to her long eyelashes.

He stared at her, transfixed. She was beautiful. So beautiful she took his breath away. His heart skipped a beat. His breath caught in his throat.

For the first time, he felt a sense of wonder. And that wonder was a feeble spark, which gradually grew into action.

He closed the distance between them.

She looked up. Her eyes were like endless voids, sucking him in, and he let himself be.

He opened his mouth. "Would you like to come with me?"

And so, they began to live together.

Like a fairy tale, too good to be true.

He found out she was a Creation within the first half hour. She had not the slightest idea how to wash, dry her hair, prepare a hot meal in the microwave, or make a bed.

So, he taught her, and she learned everything. For the first time, he felt useful. She made him useful.

He stopped her from burning the tenth saucepan he bought within the month, from melting his new shirt when ironing, from strangling herself with the sheets they washed on laundry day.

For the first time, his life had meaning.

But, as much as she learned everything, she could not learn how to feel emotions. She did not know how to laugh when she was happy or cry when she was sad. What it felt like to be boiling with rage or cringing from embarrassment.

She would never know what it felt like to helplessly fall in love.

One day, he looked at her. "I will get you a heart."

It became a vow. It became a purpose.

He began researching ways to acquire a heart, though he had no idea where to start. He pored over books, visited the black market during weekends, and sought the rumored great mages, but none managed to give him an answer. His ability was mediocre at best, barely sufficient to perform any of the forbidden spells written in the complex spell books.

He was wallowing in dismay in a bar one evening when a hooded figure approached him and said, "I have exactly what you're looking for."

He was handed an ornament that looked like it was fashioned from the unwanted parts of a machine.

Unnamed and faceless did not concern him.

All he wanted was an answer.

And that answer presented itself to him.

*

Rin's head throbbed with the Pulses that invaded her mind.

She felt his resentment, which then became resignation, and then an endless pool of longing, obsession – and something else that she could not place her finger on.

"You see, I do not think what I did was wrong. After all, I did ask for permission. They were the ones who greedily asked and readily agreed to it." His voice echoed throughout the wrecked space. "They asked for it – the ones responsible for murder are the ones who asked for it. *She is having an affair with my man – I want her dead. I hate his guts. He stole all my hard work and took all the credit – he deserves to die.* All these were fervent wishes made from their hearts. I just made it happen." He regarded them. "Tell me, would you blame the cat if the mouse ventured into its lair looking for cheese?"

Kazu rose to his feet and dusted himself off. "There's a difference between intentional and accidental."

The Manager shook his head. "There is no difference when it comes to survival. Every human heart is selfish; it is only a matter of how it is represented. The mouse chose to look for cheese in a cat's lair. The cat chose to eat the mouse. In the end, there is intent in every choice made. Who are we to judge? Every person who came to the shop intended to get something in return for their payment – be it blessing or someone else's suffering. I am just fulfilling their wishes."

Rin thought of the children trapped inside the photographs, the people trapped inside the clockwork. "There is a difference. Implicating the innocent is always wrong. They do not choose to be here. You cannot justify what you do at the expense of others."

Seeds amplified negativity. Prolonged exposure to a Territory made people prone to corruption. Some people were corrupt to begin with. Some people, however, were victims of corruption.

This man was neither. He was prey to his circumstances; he developed the mindset along the way. Morals did not apply to him.

To him, he was achieving his goals. To Rin and Kazu, he was a criminal and the Master of a Seed that had to be destroyed.

A black item glinted between the rose petals over his chest.

Rin's body reacted the moment she saw Kazu move.

A gunshot rang out.

The Sygn cluttered across the floor. The Manager fumbled for it. Rin closed in on him, blade drawn.

A blur of movement invaded her field of vision, and the edge of her blade was countered by force. A blur of silver missed her by an inch as she ducked and rammed her elbow into the assailant.

Emilia stood in front of the Manager, one hand holding a knife, the other bleeding from a long gash. She showed no signs of pain.

Rin realized belatedly that Emilia's blood was the same color as a human's.

"My dearest!" the Manager exclaimed, cradling her injured arm in his.

"Elziel?"

Rin turned.

The impact earlier landed her close to where Hayle was, and the noise seemed to have woken him up. He squinted at her and his surroundings. "Where's Rayve?"

The Sygn on the floor broke.

Nothing happened.

For a moment, Rin stared at it, her mind reeling.

The space was still falling apart. The mechanisms were still rotating, picking up speed as time passed.

She glanced over at Kazu, who mirrored her puzzlement.

The Manager glanced at Hayle and sighed. "Do you know what is the most powerful of all?"

When no one answered, he did it himself, "A wish, something you want, a Desire you would die for."

Rin's misgivings grew. It had been gnawing at her since she entered the Territory.

Hayle was picking himself up, unsteady on his feet. Awake.

A Master would usually be unaware that he was in a Territory; his mind would be trapped in a sleep-wake state, led by the Seed's illusions, and living entirely in the Territory. If the Master woke up, there would be two alternatives.

Either the Territory would disappear or the Seed would grow agitated and show itself.

"Do you..." Rin began. "Do you remember what happened?"

Hayle looked utterly confused. "What happened – I..." He shook his head. "I think I had a long dream, but I couldn't remember what it was. Why am I in a Territory?"

He was completely himself, as though freed from the Seed.

Or –

He was never under the influence of the Seed.

The Manager was smiling.

A wish... Something you would die for.

Please don't leave me alone... You're all I have.

All this while she had been assuming Hayle was the Master –
because she had been led to believe it.

She had seen him in the alley because she was *made to see it.*

"You!" she began, glaring at the Manager.

He played his cards in a way no one could tell.

"Yes, you guessed right." The Manager said, very pleased. "I am
no longer the Master."

He had given his Heart away to the Seed and was now no
different from his clients.

The actual Master was the one who lured her there and had been
acting strange while remaining unaware of it.

The person who made the trade, the person with the desire, with
the wish...

It was Rayve.

CHAPTER TWENTY-TWO

Edwin liked fighting.

He liked the fiery rush in his veins, the momentary clench of his heart, the fleeting moment of muscle-tensing preparation, followed by the spring uncoiling release. To him, it was a display of skill, a magic show, an indispensable source of inspiration to create new cards.

He had plenty of experience chasing and being chased by Seeds.

Being chased by a Territory with killing intent was a different story altogether.

He let his cards fly, releasing their magic over the mob surrounding him.

Eight of Hearts – bind. A train of cards merged to form a rope that bound five people and tripped them.

Five of Spades – cut. An invisible blade ripped through the air, slashing the incoming attackers. The defeated ones cried out, dropped their weapons, and vanished into the ground like a drop of ink falling into a sea of black.

Even the shadows were out to kill him. They stretched, lengthened, morphed from left, right, below, everywhere, reaching up his ankles and knees with probing fingers..

Nine of Diamonds – rend. The shadows trying to hold him dispersed, only to have their compatriots take their places.

Ace of Hearts – barrier. An invisible wall pushed the advancing mob back. They hammered, slashed, and tore at the wall.

He was unpleasantly reminded of the post-apocalyptic zombie movie he watched last summer with Kazu.

Exhaustion crept on him. Magic was limitless, but there was a limit to his stamina. He lost count of how long he had been repeating the similar moves over and over, and the enemies were replenishing themselves.

Where are they? he thought to himself.

The Territory was holding him back, delaying him from reaching his friends.

"Ace of Spa-"

The entire space rippled with tremendous force. For a moment, he felt light-headed.

From the edges of his vision, he saw an oozing blackness closing in.

He knew what it was.

A mature Seed that had fed enough would retract its Territory, focusing its attention and energy on its Master.

They were running out of time.

The shadowy hands gripped his pants and glued him to the spot firmly. Edwin cursed, sending out another card. The hands were faster, multiplying and latching onto him, determined to drag him in.

Blackness obscured his vision.

He found himself suspended in the still darkness.

Then, a loud gunshot rang out, followed by the sound of glass breaking.

*

For a long time, Rin had the strangest sense that she was falling.

The sensation stopped, and she was left disoriented.

In the darkness, a red spotlight snapped on, illuminating a scene straight from a horror stage play.

The Seed was a monstrosity made of gears and turning mechanisms. Two blades stuck out from it like waving arms. Terrified screams and cries rang out as men, women, and children alike were drawn toward its rotating gears. One by one, they disappeared like meat entering a mincer. Black fluid oozed out, spilling over the floor and down the platform.

The clockwork heart was consuming the townspeople.

A visual representation of what was actually happening.

"Help! Help me!" the gambling house lady cried, stretching out a hand to Rin. Black liquid poured down her forehead, sparing her terrified eyes. "I don't want to die!"

She was helplessly drawn towards the gears and vanished, her screams mingling with others.

"Rayve!"

Rin turned.

On the other side of the heart, standing in front of the gears with a vacant expression, was Rayve.

Hayle scrambled towards him, his feet slipping over the black liquid pooling on the ground.

Rayve extended his hand towards the Seed.

The screams were suddenly fuzzy noises that popped and crackled. Hayle's cries sounded far away. Everything seemed to freeze.

The Seed raised its blade-like arms and, in a single fluid motion, lobbed Rayve's head off.

Hayle let out an enraged cry. Tears streamed down his face as he charged the Seed.

A rope materialized and wrapped itself around him, stopping him in his tracks as pillars of light emerged through the cracks in the ground.

The illusion broke – Kazu's doing.

They were back in the courtyard of the apartment. The Seed hovered above the Manager. Rayve was standing in front of them. To Rin's relief, his head was intact. He wore the same vacant look. The townspeople sprawled on the ground, motionless.

"What are you doing this for?" she demanded.

The Manager laughed. His laughter echoed off the walls, a sound of exhilaration and triumph.

"Why, you ask. Because I want my beloved to know what it feels like to be loved, to be angry, hated, betrayed." He touched Emilia's face, leaving a smudge of red on her cheek. "You are as beautiful as when we first met. So empty – so much like me, yet so different. Your emptiness is pure. My emptiness is built on feelings that have been trampled, tainted, and lost."

He removed his hand and gazed at them. "Such beauty is not permissible, do you not agree?"

Rin wondered if his twisted mind was a result of the Seed's manipulation or a result of his past. Either way, it could not matter anymore.

The Seed had presented itself.

She quietly summoned a throwing knife to her hand.

"Wait," Kazu said in a low voice, frowning at the Manager. "Look."

The Manager started to bleed from the top of his head. Black as ink, the blood trickled down his chin, down his neck, running down his arms and dripping off his fingers. As they watched, he started to melt.

The Seed's mechanism clattered and clamored.

He was being absorbed by it.

Emilia stood next to him, watching with her default blank expression.

He turned to her and spoke with what was left of his mouth. "This is my gift to you, my dearest."

The moment the Seed consumed its old Master, it began rebuilding itself. The exposed mechanism gained cover. A black pillar connected the main body to the stage and flared outwards like roots. At the center of its metallic body, an eye emerged – red irises with a jet-black pupil.

A flurry of noises filled Rin's ears. Pleas, sadistic laughter, cries of resentment. She attempted to block them, but they seemed to be playing inside her head.

The repulsive force the Seed exuded as a result of the numerous hearts it devoured made Rin sick.

Kazu fired at the eye. Rayve raised a hand.

The shot was blocked by an invisible barrier.

"Rayve!" Hayle cried. "Wake up!"

"Get back!"

The Seed swung a blade arm at Hayle.

A figure sprinted forward and grabbed his collar, dragging him back as the blade slammed into the ground.

"Are you planning to die?" Edwin's angry voice rang out.

"I-" Hayle began.

"Ed, your help here will be gladly appreciated," Kazu said.

Edwin straightened himself and frowned at the Seed. "I was wondering what that terrible stench was. Turns out it's a full-fledged Seed."

Kazu reloaded his gun and fired at the barrier.

Edwin tossed Hayle aside and drew out three cards. Flinging them into the air, he called out, "Ten of Diamonds - break!"

The cards gathered, forming a translucent hammer that smashed at the barrier. Its defenses began to crumble beneath the combined weight of their abilities –

The village was on fire. Blood stained the snow. Ashes clouded the air.

A Seed stood in the middle of the ruins, holding a child in its claws.

"Leave him alone!" Rayve screamed, his voice breaking. He flung every piece of rubble and rock he could reach. "Let him go! Please!"

No one stood out to help them. No one wanted to help them.

The barrier shattered, and shards flew in all directions. Black spots flew across Rin's vision as she forced herself out of Rayve's Pulse and leaped into the air. His anguish and fear struck like knives, sharp and thorough. Her sword appeared in her hands, its obsidian blade glinting in response to her will. She twisted mid-air and brought the blade down on the Seed's exposed eye.

The force that erupted from it sent Rin reeling backward. Activating a support Magic Circle, she righted herself mid-air and readied herself to charge again.

"Rin, look out!"

It swung a blade arm down on Rin, and she raised her sword to parry. The force threw her to the other side of the courtyard. Her shoulder throbbed as she reeled backward, the tip of her sword grating the ground.

Kazu's light pillars emerged from the ground, holding the Seed in place as Edwin's magic cards slashed its blades off.

Devoid of its eye and blade arms, the Seed fell limp.

"Yes!" Edwin jubilated, readying another card.

Black spires emerged from the ground around Rayve's feet.

The night was cold and bitter. Left homeless and covered with injuries, they huddled together beside a dumpster that shielded them from the wind.

"Rayve...why are people so mean?"

Rayve wiped his tears and said resolutely, "I will protect you, Hayle. Don't be scared."

"B-But you get hurt. I don't want that..."

"It doesn't hurt." More tears came, and he wiped at them furiously.

"I want Mum and Dad..." His younger brother buried his face in his shirt, shoulders shaking.

"They're not here anymore," Rayve said, voice cracking. "But we have each other."

And I won't leave you, *he swore.* I promise.

The Seed regenerated before their very eyes.

Rayve swayed on his feet.

Unknown voices whispered endlessly into Rin's ears, distracting her. In the background, the Seed emanated a high-pitched shrill.

"Great," Edwin snarled. "Of course, parasites take everything they need from the host. Looks like we're switching targets."

Hayle grabbed his arm. "No! Don't hurt Rayve!

Edwin glared at him. "Then, tell me, how are you going to get your brother away from there? The Seed will kill him before we do."

Desperation crossed Hayle's face, unaware of the roots creeping silently around his ankle. They tightened and tugged, tripping him.

Edwin cursed.

Sensing another victim, the roots sprang into action, the shadowy tendrils rising from the ground, sharp ends glinting.

"Move it, idiot!" Edwin hollered.

The tendrils lunged at Hayle, who shut his eyes.

They stopped, hovering mid-air, seemingly uncertain.

For a moment, no one moved.

Hayle opened his eyes. Did the Seed recognize him? Or was it Rayve's instinct because he was now linked to the Seed?

This was their chance.

Hayle scrambled to his feet.

The street was filled with people going to work. No one seemed to be interested in the boy wearing patched-up clothes sitting by the pavement.

His narrowed eyes scrutinized the pedestrians, sizing them up.

An elderly lady with a large shopping bag.

A young lady in her early twenties walking her dog.

A teenager hurrying to school.

His eyes fell upon a man in a suit carrying a briefcase under his arm, talking into his phone in an agitated manner.

He found his prey.

Hayle's medicine depended on him.

He must succeed.

Edwin's cards surrounded the Seed and metamorphosed into a giant cage, reinforced by Kazu's light pillars.

"Rin! Destroy it!"

She did not need Edwin to tell her what to do. Rin generally refrained from using her ability unless necessary. There had been a time when she hated her ability.

Now, however, was a necessary moment.

A Magic Circle appeared in her hands, transforming into blue flames.

The fire every Mage recognized and feared – Sacred Fire. The fire that had the ability to destroy everything.

Hayle turned white. "Rayve – what will happen to him?"

"Whether or not you can save your twin, it's up to you," Rin said. "I told him earlier – I will destroy it all."

The flames danced around her, taking the shape of two fiery birds. They spread their wings and surged forward – eager for the kill, igniting the path they traversed. The black roots crawling over the ground serving as guidewires.

The fire ate away at the black pillar.

The Seed, sensing mortal danger – began to thrash.

A disheveled man who seemed to have forgotten to shave for half a year stood at the entrance.

"This is our home! Get out of there!"

"Says who?" the beggar mocked him, and a cacophony of laughter was heard from inside. "Blame your stupid lil' brother – he was the one who let us in."

Anger rose within Rayve. They ganged up on Hayle?

"You bastards! How dare you do this to my brother! You will pay for -"

The rest of his sentence was cut short as a blow landed on his stomach, and the wind rushed out of him. Black spots flew across his vision.

Dropping to his knees, gasping for breath, he vaguely heard Hayle say something.

Laughter and mockery rang in his ears as fists and kicks rained on his body, and he tried to shield Hayle.

"In the wilderness, only the strongest survives. There's no room for morals and values."

The flames swallowed the pillar, climbing up towards the clockwork heart. Its eye darted around frantically in its socket.

The high-pitched shrill in Rin's ears grew louder and louder. She saw Kazu covering one ear while maintaining his ability at the same time, shoulders tensed with focus.

Edwin muttered swear words that served as a mantra as he tried to add more cards to his cage.

The Seed tightened its hold on Rayve – its sole hope of survival. For as long as Rayve was trapped, they shared the same fate.

Destroying the Seed meant killing Rayve with it. And Seeds, being the cunning, manipulative beings they were, took advantage of conscience and connection, kindness, and sanity.

It was forcing out Rayve's unpleasant memories to be used as weapons against them, against him – to break him, so that it could have all of him.

He stood at the counter of the Heart Shop and stared at the form.

He knew it was a Seed. But he could not resist.

"Will you be able to save my brother?"

"It depends on how much you are willing to offer."

He would do anything for Hayle. "I'll give you as much as you need."

Hayle flung himself onto Rayve. "I'm sorry you have to shoulder everything by yourself. I'm sorry you had to suffer because of me! I knew all this while I knew you were protecting me."

"Master, he'll be all right, won't he?"

"Hayle is strong. Don't worry, dear boy."

"The Seed got him when I wasn't looking. I –" He was unable to complete his sentence.

"It's all right now. Your brother will be fine. What happened to the Seed?"

Rayve clenched his fists. "I killed it."

"I'm sorry!" Hayle sobbed. "I'm really sorry for giving you trouble. You've done enough. Please stop."

Why are you sorry? Why are you apologizing?

Rin's head felt like it was about to burst.

The Seed retaliated with a tremendous wave of energy that threw Kazu and Edwin off their feet.

She glanced at Rayve. If he was unable to regain his senses –

The tendrils snaked around Kazu and Edwin's necks, attempting to strangle them to free itself.

The flames reached Rayve's knees.

Dread drenched her heart. She did not want to kill another person.

But if she released her flames, Kazu and Ed would –

I will kill anything or anyone that tries to harm you.

Hayle threw his head back and screamed, "Wake up, you idiot! Look at me!"

Rayve's eyes came into focus.

"Hayle?"

Rayve's voice was barely audible above all the noise, but the Seed was proof – it faltered. "Why are you here?" He rasped, "What's going on?"

Hayle let out a sob and hugged his older brother. "Let's go home," he said. "Together."

The tendrils around their feet loosened, and the black spires vanished.

The flames climbed up to the heart of the Seed, eating away its body, eye, and everything.

Until there was nothing left.

Rayve dropped to his knees. He raised his head weakly. "Why are you crying?"

Hayle did not answer.

It started to rain. Small droplets gradually became a shower, pouring over the remnants of the Sacred Fire. Rin found herself lying on her back, unable to move. Between the lines of her blurry vision, she saw a figure step onto the platform where the bright red core of the Seed hovered, unattended.

She blinked, trying to make out who it was.

The figure disappeared.

The core of the Seed was nowhere to be seen.

So was the Creation.

CHAPTER TWENTY-THREE

Two days had passed since the encounter with the full-fledged Seed.

Cnaris was very displeased. He had to file a report to the Council because it was not an assigned task.

"Do you know how much paperwork I have to hand in?" he complained and descended into a half-hour-long tirade before spending the rest of the day in a foul temper.

Rin chose to escape. The afterimages of the burning town and the mechanical heart settled at the back of her mind like unwanted residue alongside the exhaustion that lingered even after an entire day of rest.

The Signon twins were recuperating in the Council hospital. Hayle – after sending her a paragraph of gratitude – had developed a tendency to chat with her, sending her texts now and then as though they were close friends.

The children trapped in the toy emporium were rescued and reunited with their families. The note that had arrived at her doorstep vanished along with the Seed – without a trace.

Osmanthus Street was gone.

The people of Pallin were made to believe that it was an abandoned place after a fire broke out many years ago.

The Seed's influence spread like an irremovable plague that slowly planted roots in the hearts and minds of the townspeople and finally consumed them in their entirety. The non-refundable rule of the Heart Shop applied till the very end. There were many whose hearts were beyond salvaging, having sunken too deep into the abyss to be recovered. The Council searched the entire street, but all they found was old furniture and the remnants of belongings of the people who once lived there.

They're long gone, Rin thought. Traded their hearts right down to the very last strands of their souls.

Those who took part in trades but did not lose all their hearts to the Seed were taken into custody by the Council. There had been no news of them since. The Council was determined to cover up the incident and made those involved swear a non-disclosure oath.

The presence of a Seed that was allowed to fester for such long periods, dealing irreparable damage to a community, left a bitter aftertaste. She wasn't sure how much of it was their own will, or how much their wills were distorted by the presence of the Seed.

But wills were only easily bent if they were made that way.

On the third day, Kazu and Edwin dropped by. Cnaris greeted them with a look reminiscent of a ferocious pit bull – one that would have made cats flee across three yards. Mirelle stepped to their rescue and ushered him into his study.

The three of them lounged in Rin's room with Mirelle's signature shortbread and tea.

"In the end, he gained nothing from it. He wanted her to feel the pain and the resentment he felt, but," Edwin said, biting into a shortbread, "he was gambling against the impossible. She didn't even shed a tear when he died."

"Maybe he just wanted to have a sense of purpose, and the Seed made use of that purpose against him, changing the original intent," Kazu said, resting his chin against his hand.

Edwin shook his head. "Oh, I don't know. He could have just been a sadistic bastard from the start."

Emilia was nowhere to be found. No one had spotted the mysterious man who collected the Seed's core, either.

Rin glanced at Kazu, who was gazing out the windows, lost in thought. She recalled what he said about the sisters, how they called themselves people of Reverse.

Reverse – a name from children's books. Rei used to read them to her when she was younger. She recalled not liking them for an unknown reason, and he stopped, but the story stuck somehow. It referred to the magic that was believed to govern time and space. Magic that recorded every event of the past and present. The character of the story tried to change the past by rewriting the story, but he got the sequel wrong, affecting others and eventually destroying the world.

It was dark, as far as children's stories were concerned.

Rin wondered if it was the Reverse they meant. There had to be people who revered that kind of magic. After all, the acceptance of Seeds meant the refusal to acknowledge the past and the denial of the bitterness of the present.

It was hard to imagine that someone was out there making Seeds and giving them out like souvenirs.

"Do you think..." Rin began. They both turned to her. "That there might be a link between Seeds and Reverse?"

"Who knows? Even the Council doesn't appear to know," Edwin said, playing with the loose threads at the edge of the cushion, rocking his chair on its two front legs.

Or maybe they just didn't want to reveal what they knew. After all, the Council held their secrets close. Hunters were only those in the outer rings, taking up jobs offered and carrying out their commands.

There was a brief silence.

Then, Edwin spoke. "We could've made a fortune if we destroyed the Seed's core."

Kazu nearly spat his tea. "*That's* what you're thinking about?"

"You only care about money, don't you?"

"Well, money is the essence of well-being, cat." Edwin prodded Rin with shortbread, spilling crumbs over her sleeve. "Speaking of which, what did you trade at the Heart Shop?"

Kazu put his cup down, clearly interested.

Rin made a noncommittal gesture. "I asked for my father to stop bothering me with extra classes."

"*What?*" Edwin's chair teetered dangerously. "Are you for real? You give away a portion of your heart for *that?*" He burst out laughing.

"Shut up." Rin flung a cushion at him, feeling heat rise in her face.

Kazu worked hard to keep his face straight. "I guess everyone has different views as to what holds value to them. So, did it work?"

"I don't know. He just hasn't..." Rin broke off and glared at them. "Look, I was just testing it out. I couldn't possibly ask for something really important." She kicked Edwin's chair. "What would *you* ask for, then?"

"Me? I would've asked for a big house, complete with a garden, a pool..." Edwin thought for a moment before adding, "And a casino on the top floor. It shall rival the Lent house, and I'll be able to host casino parties-"

"And you'll end up heartless because it'll cost a fortune," Rin snapped.

"I thought you said it depends on how much value it has to you."

"I think greed was the cause of the downfall," Kazu began.

"He's saying you're greedy."

Edwin let his chair fell onto all fours and shrugged. "I call it creativity. Yours is so bland he probably saw through you from the very start. How does it feel to lack one out of a hundredth of your heart?"

Rin nearly threw another cushion in his face. "I don't think it granted my wish, so I probably didn't lose anything."

Outside, the sun started to set, casting an orange glow on the furniture. Mirelle came to invite them to dinner and just in time to stop cushions from being ripped apart.

Rin stayed back a little longer to tidy up. Her phone lit up – probably another text from Hayle.

The Seed had disappeared, but deep down, the feeling of unfinished business nagged at her.

EPILOGUE

In the outskirts of an obscure town far to the east, four figures trod along the ragged cobblestone path. Three of them wore identical cloaks: black with large hoods that hid their visages.

"Hey, Ceci, why did you spare them? You even spilled the beans about us."

Cecila turned a note containing directions in her hands and glanced at the quaint buildings they walked past. "It doesn't matter. They will find out soon. After all, if we did something out of step with *his* plans, *he* would not be happy about it. What do you think will happen?"

Jessabelle gasped and clutched her neck, rolling her eyes and making gagging sounds.

What a drama queen.

"That blonde guy is really cute," Jessabelle said dreamily. "I hope we'll see him again."

"I daresay we will," Cecila said impatiently to shut her up and turned to Quantum, who was dragging his feet behind them. "We are behind schedule. Would you please walk faster?"

"I'm tired... How about you two carry me?"

Jessabelle sniggered. "Master Quantum is great at telling jokes."

"He isn't," Cecila snapped. "That is not a joke."

She stopped in front of a nameless run-down bar. A faded *OPEN* sign hung at the doors.

There was nothing special about this place. It looked too ordinary. Maybe it had been chosen for that reason. Maybe there was nostalgic value behind its antique walls – of course, there was also a chance that it was because Master Imp couldn't *see*.

Whatever the reason was, it was not hers to ponder.

She entered first, holding the door open for Quantum to lumber through.

The bar was empty except for the collection of cobwebs at the corners, an array of old tables stacked against the side walls, and a couple of chairs lying akimbo on the dusty wooden floor.

Sitting at the counter was a small child-like figure, clad in the same black cloak.

"Quantum, you're late." The voice was soft, with a silky, intangible quality that could easily slip between fingers.

Walking up to him, Cecila bowed and said, "Apologies, Master Imp. There was an unforeseen event with the client. He was...a lot more trouble than expected."

"But you pulled through." The child enunciated every word.

As he spoke, time seemed to slow down. Cecila found herself falling into his pace.

She carefully placed an object wrapped in cloth on the counter.

"Good work."

"We thought it was impossible to get it back!" Jessabelle flailed her arms in excitement.

"Now that we're done," Quantum drawled, "do I get to take a nap?"

Cecila gave him a withering look. "That's all you've been doing the entire year we were there." To the child, she said, "Master Imp, we also brought someone back."

Imp turned his head slightly. "A Creation."

Cecila was secretly very impressed.

He lacks vision, yet he sees.

Jessabelle pranced in front of Emilia, the latter not showing any emotion. "You're coming home. Aren't you happy? Oops, I forgot. Creations can't feel." She cackled. "After all, the foolish man did to give you a *heart -*"

Quantum let out a loud, obnoxious yawn.

Emilia inclined her head in a polite bow. "Greetings, Masters."

"So, you do remember your origin." Imp's unseeing eyes swept past her and rested upon the empty air next to her. Then, he slid off his seat. "Let's go."

"Where to?" Quantum whined.

"Back to where we belong."

ACKNOWLEDGMENTS

This is a very important instalment because it is the first of the many volumes to come in the future. I would like to thank the numerous hands who extended their help to make the launch of this project possible.

To my beta-readers, KY, Jiann, Sabbie, WY and Sam – the first ones to read the story, your feedbacks are invaluable to me. For your time, your effort and your motivational words, you have my utmost gratitude.

To my editor and lifesaver, Clara, your critical mind and sharp eyes fixed many loopholes and added much strength to the plot. Thank you for bearing with my numerous errors, typos, and awkward word choices.

To Abir, for saving me from the struggle of website designing. To Zaryab, for writing up a marketing strategy – something that I have no idea about. To windmill72 for creating the animated project logo many, many years ago.

To my parents, friends and supporters on social media, to the strangers who visited my booth during art conventions and expressed your interest in this project. You have no idea how much those moments mean to me.

And lastly, to you, for reading this book to the end.

Thank you from the bottom of my heart.